Subhadra Sen Gupta has written over forty books for children because she thinks children are the best readers in the world. She loves telling stories woven aorund history; plotting complicated mysteries and crazy adventures; dreaming up ghostly tales and scripting comic books. In 2014 she was awarded the Bal Sahitya Puraskar by the Sahitya Akademi for her children's books. If you want to start a conversation with her, send her an email here and she promises to reply: subhadrasg@gmail.com.

Also by Subhadra Sen Gupta in Talking Cub

The Teenage Diary of Jodh Bai (2019)
The Teenage Diary of Jahanara (2019)

MOSTLY GHOSTLY STORIES

SUBHADRA SEN GUPTA

talking
CUB

An Imprint of Speaking Tiger Books

TALKING CUB
Published by Speaking Tiger Books LLP
4381/4, Ansari Road, Daryaganj
New Delhi 110002

First published in paperback in Talking Cub by Speaking Tiger
Books in 2019

ISBN: 978-93-89231-60-1
eISBN: 978-93-89231-59-5

10 9 8 7 6 5 4 3 2 1

CONTENTS

AJJi'S ABACUS

'You are getting it all wrong again, Durga!'
'I am NOT, Ajji!'

The air around my head felt like a dozen birds were angrily flapping their wings, and then the pesky bees began buzzing softly in my ears.

Ajji was becoming agitated and soon I was going to get a headache.

'You can't overcharge the customers! It is bad for business... I've told you so many times,' Ajji was hissing in my ears. 'It will be one silver tara and six copper jital coins. Can't you even add a simple bill?'

'Yes, I know that...'

'Didn't you see Keshava serve eight dosas, six helpings of bisi bele bhaat, and then six coconut payasams? How much does that add up to?'

'I know! One tara and six jitals but Ajji, they have just now asked for six paans. So I added two jitals.'

'Ohh…' There was a small silence as Ajji's soft deflated exclamation fluttered around my head. My grandmother hated being proved wrong.

I turned slightly and spoke to the empty air behind me, knowing she was listening, 'You know Ajji, I never make mistakes adding up a bill.' I couldn't help smiling. It always felt good being one up on her. 'I am your granddaughter, remember?'

'Don't forget to give them the correct change,' she said briskly. My bossy grandma was never going to admit that she made a mistake.

'I will right away.'

The fluttering and buzzing suddenly died down and with relief I knew she was gone.

My younger brother Keshava who was serving the customers came back with the payment, took a look at my glum face and grinned, 'Finding mistakes, was she?'

Busy counting the coins I just nodded. 'You should hear her when I am making the bill,' he wiped his sweaty face with a cloth. 'It's like a hundred angry bees buzzing in my ears.'

'I don't blame her. You and Appa are terrible at even the simplest additions and subtractions.'

'And aren't you clever!' He grabbed the change and went off looking hopeful. The customers were a bunch of rich noblemen from Thanjavur and my optimistic brother was hoping for a tip.

My best friend Pampa says we are the strangest family in Vijayanagar. The men do the cooking and serving and the women count the money. Ajji and Amma are champions at numbers; I'm pretty good at it, too, while Appa and Keshava are truly talented cooks. So we are sort of an upside down family because Appa and Keshava begin to sweat if they have to calculate the expenses of a small shopping list, while Amma and I are pretty good at burning a whole pot of sambar.

If we are strange, you have to blame Ajji for that.

Actually, in our family everything begins with Ajji. At one time, my grandmother, Sundari Ammal, was an important member of the staff at the palace of Krishna Deva Raya, the king of Vijayanagar. When she entered the palace, the guards at the gate bowed to her and greeted her respectfully by saying, 'Namaskara, Sundari Ammal!' and she would sweep by with a regal nod. She was one of the most trusted officers in the zenana—the complex of palaces of the queens of Vijayanagar. Ajji was the Chief Accountant who managed all the expenses, and in the thirty years that she had served the royal family no one ever found a mistake in her calculations.

I remember going with Amma to visit her in the zenana. She sat in a small room, cross-legged on a mattress on the floor, with a bolster at her back; before her was a low table and she was surrounded by bundles of palm leaf. She was clacking away at her abacus, then dipping her quill pen into a pot of ink and writing down the endless rows of numbers. I peered over her shoulder to see what she was writing and read a long list:

Purchase of oil for lamps.
Cost of repairing wall in kitchen.
Allowance to Queen Padmalaya.
Loan to Head Gardener.

And against each expense, the row of numbers, all of them neatly added at the bottom. The way I love to do.

As Ajji began to grow old her eyes became weak and her hands began to shake and that was when Amma began to help her. But when it came to the calculations… click… clack… Ajji always used the abacus and she had the correct answer. Every time.

She bought the abacus from a merchant from a far-off land. He had come with a trunk full of lengths of shimmering silks. As the women in the zenana crowded around him buying the silks, Ajji had watched him calculate the price on his abacus, quickly shifting the row of beads in the wooden frame.

The merchant had raised his slanted eyes and asked Ajji, 'And you, Madam? Don't you want the silks of China?'

'No.' Ajji pointed to the abacus. 'I want that machine.'

The man laughed, 'It is not for sale.'

'Everything is for sale,' said Ajji firmly, 'name your price.'

Amused at a woman wanting an abacus, the man had bargained and then sold it to Ajji. Then he had taught her how to use it and watched in amazement as within a few minutes she was calculating faster than him.

'You are very good with numbers, Madam,' the man said admiringly. 'You should run your own business.'

'I run this palace,' she snapped at him and stalked away to her office carrying her prize. From then the abacus never left her side.

Everyone working in the zenana said that after Ajji got the abacus she became a complete terror. She found mistakes in everyone's bills and began adding interest to the loans. And if they protested she would say that her abacus was never wrong. Then she did the same at Appa's food shop. She declared that Appa spent too much on kitchen supplies, overpaid the servants and calculated everything wrong. After a session with Ajji and her abacus Appa would walk away red-faced and muttering under his breath that one day he would drop that 'devil's machine' in the kitchen fire.

When Ajji retired from her job as the Chief Accountant of the zenana, she was summoned to the palace of His Majesty, King Krishna Deva Raya. As she bowed and touched his feet, he raised her up with a smile and said, 'Ah, Sundari Ammal! What will I do without you? Who will manage the zenana now?'

'I am getting old, Your Majesty. The eyes ache and my hands shake. It is time for a younger woman to take over the job.'

'Oh I know who that will be. The next manager of the zenana has already been selected.' And the two exchanged a smile because Ajji knew very well who was going to take over from her. She had trained her successor well.

That is how Parvati Ammal, my Amma and Ajji's daughter, took over the running of the zenana. And Ajji retired so that she could run Appa's life instead.

Appa had a food shop in Hampi Bazaar, the broad avenue that ran from the high gopuram gateway of the Virupaksha Temple to the Matanga Hill, with shops on both sides. It was the busiest bazaar in Vijayanagar. Pilgrims came from far to do puja at this ancient shrine of Lord Shiva and many would come to eat in our food shop. Appa thought his business was doing very well but Ajji had different ideas.

Ajji always planned her life carefully. Over the years she had saved money and with it she now bought the best spot in Hampi Bazaar and opened an inn and food shop, right in front of the main gate of the Virupaksha Temple. Soon the inn was the most popular in the city, its rooms always full and its food shop packed with hungry pilgrims. As my brother Keshava and I grew up, we began to help Appa, carrying in the brass plates of food, shopping for vegetables, cleaning and dusting the rooms in the inn.

Life was good. We lived on top of the inn and every morning Amma headed off to the palace and came back in the late afternoon. Appa would be up at dawn and whirling around the kitchen yelling at the cooks and waiters. Keshava and I served at the food shop and cleaned the rooms in the inn. Ajji made the bills, her fingers flying over the abacus and then dropping the coins into the money box with a happy clatter.

When I was sixteen and Keshava two years younger, our simple world fell apart. Suddenly, Sundari Ammal, my Ajji, died.

But she did not go away.

A few days after Ajji's funeral, I was loitering on the top floor when I heard Amma and Appa talking on the terrace below.

'Without her,' Appa was saying, 'what will I do? I can't run the inn and the food shop alone. And as your mother said so often, I'm a good cook but I have no head for business.' He gave a sad little laugh. 'I fought with her all the time and now I miss her…'

There was a small silence and then Amma said, 'If you want me to, I can stop working at the palace…'

'Oh no!' Appa exclaimed. 'His Majesty chose you

for the job and Queen Tirumale Devi trusts you. We cannot risk the royal family becoming angry with us. Also, you are paid so well.'

'And,' Amma said softly, 'I love the work. Just like my mother did. It gives me joy.'

I stood there scratching my nose and thinking hard. I thought of how I loved our inn. Right across the road I could see the stone and stucco gopuram gateway and the row of shacks selling flowers, coconuts, bananas, incense, brass utensils for the pilgrims coming to perform puja. People were walking down the steps of the temple tank to take a purifying dip before heading to the sanctum with their platters of offerings for the gods and goddesses. I could hear Chinappa, the blind beggar, calling out to the pilgrims from his spot by the main courtyard; I remembered I had to take him some food.

This was my world, I thought absently. Ajji had built it for us and we had to hold on to it. Appa could not do it alone.

In our family, all discussions happen over dinner when the day's work is done, the food shop closed and the guests of the inn tucked into their rooms. Then we can relax. Keshava and I lay out the cloth seats on the floor of the empty kitchen and place the metal plates as Appa and Amma carry the leftover food— the kosambari salad, the vegetables, the vadas… and sometimes if we are lucky some sweets too—kesari bhaat or payasam.

As we start to eat Amma always asks two questions, 'How was business at the food shop?' Then, 'Any new guests at the inn?'

One day, a few months after Ajji died, we were at dinner and Amma again wanted to know if we had any new guests.

'Two guests,' Keshava said. 'They have come with saris from Kanchipuram.'

I took a deep breath and spoke, 'I did the bills today.' Amma looked up. 'The food shop was so full and Appa was so busy…'

Amma frowned, looking uncannily like Ajji, '*All* the bills?'

Munching a vada I gave a full report of my activities that day, 'I sat with the vegetable seller and calculated and cleared his bills. Ajji always bargained with him and he was so happy I did not, that he gave me a pumpkin for free.'

Appa laughed, Keshava was grinning but Amma still frowned.

'Two guests left and I did their bills.'

'Then Akka sat in the food shop and collected all the money from the customers,' Keshava sprang to my aid.

'No mistakes, no one complained and that's because I used the abacus.'

By now even Amma was smiling. 'She taught you how to use it, didn't she?'

So from then on I became the business manager of the inn. In the beginning, Amma would check my calculations every night but after a few months she began to trust me and that is because she couldn't spot a single mistake. Best of all, I became very popular with all the people who supplied goods to the inn— the grocer, the vegetable and fruit sellers, the man who made ghee and even the bad-tempered washerman. This was because, unlike Ajji, I did not bargain, say rude things about their goods or snap their heads off if they argued. Then when I found the money to buy expensive spices and new frying pans for the kitchen, Appa said that I was a better manager than Ajji. And that made Amma laugh.

What I did not know was that Ajji did not approve of my business style.

Every evening before dinner, I would sit and make a final list of all the earnings and expenses of the day to show to Amma and Appa. One evening, I sat by the light of two earthen lamps, scratching away with my quill pen in my red cloth-covered register and rattling the beads of the abacus. It was a hot summer night when suddenly I felt a cool breeze around my head. I looked around to see who was fanning me. There was no one around.

Then she whispered in my ear and her voice seemed to be coming from far, far away, 'Very little profit today.'

'Uh!' I sat frozen in panic.

'Just two silver taras and six jitals, that is not good.' The voice was getting stronger.

'Ajji? Is that you?' I whispered nervously, my heart thudding, 'Are you *alive*?'

'Don't be silly, girl! I died, remember?' she snapped at me as I sat very still, thinking if I moved too much she would somehow vanish like a dream. 'But I did not go away. I have been here all the time.'

'Really?' I was not amused. 'You died two months ago, how come you did not speak to me before? Not even *once*?'

'Because you were doing a good job.'

'Oh, was I?' I glared in the direction of a window from where I sensed her voice was coming. 'Then what's gone wrong today?'

'Three guests pay their bills, the food shop was full and just two taras and six jitals in profit? What kind of business is that?'

'There were expenses,' I said a little defensively.

'Of course! You paid off the full bill of that stupid washerman Chandramouli!' Ajji was always fighting with the poor man.

'Ajji, his daughter is getting married and I asked Appa first.'

'Tchuk!' she made her typical clicking noise of disapproval and now I was absolutely sure I was speaking to my grandma. 'Your Appa will give away my inn to a beggar one day because the beggar sang so well. You never clear all their dues, you stupid girl. Never! Keep them waiting.'

'I won't!' I was feeling pretty stubborn too. 'Why should I, when I have the money and they are all so poor?'

'Tchuk! I shouldn't have taught you the abacus.'

The breeze died down and Ajji was gone.

I realized that if things went smoothly at the inn Ajji was quiet. Then one day when Keshava did the billing because I was ill, he made a pile of mistakes and Ajji arrived to yell into his ears. There was a full orchestra of buzzing bees accompanying her yelling. We never told Amma and Appa about it, because who would believe us? You hear of ghosts haunting old buildings, living in trees, wandering around temples... whoever heard of a ghost who haunted the office of an inn? Ajji never visited the kitchen or Appa would have definitely heard her sarcastic comments. She did not check the rooms in the inn or the servants would have heard her complaining about the dusting and mopping. She just watched and haunted me as I sat at her place on the divan, using her pens, ink and paper and calculating on her abacus.

One day, when she had been particularly troublesome, muttering about how Appa should raise the rent; why was I buying expensive vegetables that were out of season; did Keshava have to fill the bowls of food to the brim… I finally had to protest.

'Ajji, do you live in this room just to give me a headache?'

'Of course not! I only come when you call me.'

'Call you? I never call you. How can I call you when I can't even see you?'

'I hear the abacus and I know you are there and then I come back.'

Suddenly there was a lump in my throat and my eyes were wet with tears, 'Oh I miss you so much Ajji!'

'I know, my Durga. I know. That is why I stay.'

✦

Early one morning in the month of Kartik my friend Pampa and I, carrying bundles of clothes to be washed, walked to the Tungabhadra River for a bath. Keshava and Pampa's younger brother Ranga were strolling along ahead of us carrying the brass pots in which they would bring back the river water to be used for drinking at home. Our mornings began like this every day.

Pampa's father Raghavendra was the head priest at the Virupaksha Temple and he and Appa were childhood friends. As Appa jokes, he takes care of people's stomachs while his friend Raghu takes care of their souls. We four had grown up together as they lived near our inn, down the lane, in the priest's house. Pampa and I loved going for the river bath together, telling each other all the private things that only a friend will understand. It was the same with Keshava and Ranga. They even knew about Ajji's ghost. You can't hide such an amazing thing from friends.

We can easily have a bath in the temple tank but the river is a living thing, its slightly chilly water flowing around our bodies in a slow, gentle way. There are boulders strewn along the bank and midstream, from where our idiotic brothers love to jump off and splash about. Vijayanagar has hills of huge red-gold boulders, and it seems as if a long time ago a mythical giant had played with stones here. Amma says there is so much stone everywhere that our sculptors just have to walk out of their homes and start carving—and it is true. Everywhere the boulders have beautiful images carved on them—Ganeshas and dancing girls; elephants and horses and my favourite, a Hanuman with his tail curved over his head.

Pampa calls the Tungabhadra 'my river' because the river goddess is also called Pampa. It is said that Devi Pampa prayed to Lord Shiva and he came down to earth to marry her. That is why one of the ancient names of Vijayanagar is Pampakshetra. At the city's biggest temple Lord Shiva is worshipped as Virupaksha, or 'the god with the slanted eyes' and beside him are his two consorts Devi Pampa and Devi Bhuvaneshwari. My friend was born at the time when Uncle Raghu took over as the head priest, so naturally he named his daughter Pampa.

We laid out the clothes to dry on the sandy bank of the river and sat on the stone steps before the Kodandarama Temple. I noticed that Pampa was very quiet. I can always sense when she is not happy.

'What's the matter? Had a fight with your Amma again?' I asked half-jokingly.

She shook her head, 'I don't know… something is wrong.'

'Wrong?' I turned to stare at her.

'Yesterday when Appa came home after the evening arati, he went into their room, called Amma inside and closed the door. They were talking for a long time and when they came out I saw that Amma was crying.'

'Crying? Why?'

'I don't know!' Padma stared broodingly across the river. 'When I asked her if anything was wrong, she wouldn't tell me. All through dinner Appa was silent, he did not say a word and he hardly ate anything.'

'Uncle Raghu was *quiet*?' I asked startled. He was one of the most talkative people I knew, always full of stories and jokes.

'This morning when I woke up, it was barely light but Appa had already left for the temple and Amma was in the puja room praying.' She turned to stare worriedly at me. 'Durga, they look scared. It feels like something is very wrong.'

'I don't think Appa and Amma know anything,' I said thoughtfully. 'Everything was pretty normal yesterday.'

'How do we find out?'

'I don't know.'

I looked at our brothers. Unaware of the dark clouds gathering on the horizon, they were happily yelling, diving and splashing away.

All day I kept an eye on Appa and he was his usual self. Then after lunch I saw Uncle Raghu enter the kitchen and say something to Appa; the two of them went into an empty room in the inn and closed the door behind them. I crept close to the window next to the door that was half-open and tried to listen.

They were talking in low, hurried voices and I only caught snatches of their conversation.

Uncle Raghu was saying, '… no one knows so far… the treasury was checked many times. Last month I…'

Then Appa asked, '… keys?'

'… people but I am responsible… I am sure the necklaces were there… how was I to know that…'

Papa spoke again, 'We have to…'

And then Uncle Raghu's voice rose in fear and panic, 'Dussehra is just a fortnight away! How can I tell His Majesty that they are missing from my treasury!'

I heard Appa open the bolt of the door and I quickly slipped away.

Pampa dropped in after lunch when she knew I would be free and I told her what I had heard. 'Necklaces missing from the temple treasury?' Her eyes widened in panic. 'Oh, Appa is in serious trouble! He is the head priest.'

'What is kept in the treasury? Money?'

She shook her head. 'The money that is collected at the temple every day is managed by the cashier and kept in an iron strong box in his office. The treasury has the jewellery and the royal offerings.'

'Whose jewellery is it?'

'The god and the two goddesses. We have three shrines, remember? There is the main shrine with the Shiva lingam of Lord Virupaksha. Next to it are the shrines of Devi Pampa and Devi Bhuvaneshwari.'

'Oh right! And the goddesses wear jewellery.'

'Lots of it, from the tops of their heads to their ankles—crowns, hair ornaments, earrings, armlets, bangles, necklaces, anklets and nose rings. All of it is in gold set with precious jewels like diamonds, rubies, emeralds and pearls.'

'And Uncle Raghu is responsible for them?'

'He is the head priest and only he has the keys to the treasury. Once a month he opens the treasury and checks all the jewellery against a list. Nothing has ever gone missing before.'

'But the jewellery belongs to the temple. Why does he have to tell the king that anything is missing?'

'Because Lord Virupaksha and Devi Pampa are the family deities of the king. Most of the jewellery and gifts like gold coins have been given by the royal family. Remember the time His Majesty defeated Bijapur?'

'Oh yes I remember!' I said dreamily. 'It was such an amazing celebration.'

A few months back our king Krishna Deva Raya had defeated our greatest enemy, the kingdom of Bijapur, at Raichur. When the army returned to Vijayanagar in triumph, there were processions of marching soldiers, devadasis dancing before the king's chariot, swaying elephants and prancing horses parading from the king's palace to the temple. There the king and his two queens, Tirumale Devi and Chinna Devi had worshipped the deities. His Majesty had poured gold coins over the Shiva lingam and the queens put huge gold necklaces glittering with diamonds and rubies around the necks of the goddesses.

'Two weeks from now,' Pampa said, 'the Dussehra festival will start. Before a festival the clothes and the jewellery of the goddesses are changed. If any jewellery is missing when the royal family comes to the temple on Mahanavami night… Oh my lord! Then Appa's life is in peril.'

I couldn't even say that the problem will go away. I had heard the fear in Uncle Raghu's voice. The Mahanavami puja was very important to the king as he was a religious man and an angry king could order the worst punishment.

If Uncle Raghu thought things could be kept quiet, he was mistaken. Too many people in the temple had guessed that something was wrong and by the next day the whispers had begun. I heard the gossip in the kitchen.

One of the cooks said, 'Have you heard? There has been a burglary in the temple.'

Someone asked, 'What's been stolen?'

'I think money from the cash box.'

'I heard they broke into the treasury.'

Then Appa came in and they all fell silent.

I knew who would have the news. As I did every day, after lunch I put some leftover rice and vegetables on an earthen plate and crossed the lane to enter the temple. The gopuram gateway led into the first courtyard surrounded by temple offices and rest rooms. Here by the door of the main office, Chinappa the blind beggar sat and called out to the pilgrims all day, 'Amma! Give a coin to this poor blind man and Devi Pampa will bless you!'

I put the plate before him and guided his hand to the food. 'Lunch, Grandpa. There's some brinjal curry that you like.'

He turned his milky eyes towards me with a toothless smile. 'Durgamma! You never forget this old man.'

'Never! How can I? You are my friend.'

He was hungry and began to eat quickly, as I leaned against a pillar and looked around. This was a scene I never tired of watching. The courtyard with the huge, shady, peepal tree in the middle and the pillared hall across the office were all crowded with pilgrims. The festival season had begun and they came from all around the city and the nearby villages.

Children in bright clothes were playing everywhere, ignoring their mothers calling out to them. Women sat gossiping under the tree as vendors tried to tempt them with their wares of fruits and sweets, cheap jewellery and wooden combs, saris and bright toys. Some people were taking a quick nap in the hall while others were clapping and singing hymns in praise of Shiva. It was a busy, happy place, bright with colours, all glittering in the sun.

I helped Chinappa wash his hands and then asked, 'Grandpa, is something wrong at the temple? Have you heard anything?'

Chinappa was blind but he had very sharp ears and heard everything around him. Sitting by the door of the temple office he heard what people were saying inside and also what they were talking about as they waited at the door. Often people forgot the old beggar and would talk freely, so he heard everything. Sometimes Chinappa knew the latest gossip even before Uncle Raghu did.

'Who said anything?' he frowned.

'The cooks were talking.'

'I heard something,' his face was solemn and sad because he liked Uncle Raghu.

'Raghavendra Swami is in trouble. There has been a theft in the treasury.'

'What's been stolen?'

'Two gold necklaces set with diamonds and rubies that the queens had presented to the goddesses after the victory over Bijapur.'

'How could they be missing? I thought Uncle Raghu checked the treasury every month. Wouldn't he have noticed if they were missing?'

'They were not missing.'

'What?'

'The necklaces had been replaced with fake ones. When Raghavendra checked the boxes they were there. How was he to know they were fake?'

'How did they find out they were fake?'

'Dussehra is coming, so the temple jeweller was brought in to polish the jewellery and he found that the diamonds and rubies were glass!' Chinappa shook his bald head. 'Stealing sacred jewellery! What is the world coming to?'

I got up, picking up the plate and water bowl. 'I have to talk to Appa and Amma.'

'You do that. Your Amma is a clever woman. Maybe she can solve the mystery.'

Walking home I thought, 'And I have to talk to Ajji. She had the mind of a policeman. Appa and Uncle Raghu will be useless at finding a thief, Appa just gets excited and Uncle Raghu is too upset. Ajji will know what to ask.'

At dinner, Appa told us that Uncle Raghu was summoned by Chief Minister Saluva Timma and told to find the necklaces and catch the thieves immediately. If the goddesses were not wearing the new necklaces on Mahanavami night when the king came to worship, then nothing could save him.

Amma sighed, 'Oh, I wish my Amma was here. She caught so many thieves in the zenana—a maid who stole earrings; a guard who broke into the cashier's strong box and a princess who stole the bangles of another princess because they had a fight. Amma was fearless and she caught them all.'

Appa grinned, 'She also caught the cook who liked to eat mangoes and the waiter who would somehow forget to return the change to customers. Remember how she held his dhoti and checked his pockets?'

I got up. 'Amma will you clear the plates please? I have to finish the day's bills. Four guests are leaving early tomorrow morning.'

As Keshava got up and followed me, Appa asked, 'And where are you going?'

'I am learning to use the abacus.'

I did have bills to add up and Keshava sat bent over the abacus shifting the beads back and forth with a puzzled frown. I listened to my parents put the plates and bowls for washing at the washing up place, close the doors of the food shop and kitchen, and then I heard their bedroom door close.

Keshava looked up. 'Ajji? You there?'

'Where else will I be with you fooling around with my abacus?' She was right there beside us.

'Ajji, we need your help…' I began and then told her everything.

She listened in silence and then said, 'How can such a thing happen? It is the temple treasury! What were those lazy guards doing?'

'Pampa says there are two guards at the door night and day.'

There was a thoughtful silence and I could easily imagine Ajji's ghostly brain clicking away like her abacus. 'Tell Pampa to ask Raghu two questions…'

Keshava raised his head. 'Only two questions, Ajji?'

'Yes, stupid one! First, when were the necklaces

placed in the treasury? Second, we need the names of all the people who entered the treasury after that.'

'Suppose ten people have gone into the treasury, how will we know who is the thief?' Keshava was in an argumentative mood.

'Stop arguing and do what I say!'

And Ajji was gone.

Next morning at dawn, we had quick baths and then sat talking by the river. This was not a day for swimming and diving.

'Ajji wants to know when the necklaces were placed in the treasury,' I began. 'And who entered the treasury after that. Can you ask Uncle Raghu?'

Before Pampa could reply, Ranga sat up. 'I know the answers to both questions!'

We stared at Ranga in surprise. He was the youngest amongst us, just nine years old, and he usually followed Keshava everywhere like a loyal puppy.

'You do?' I asked. 'How?'

'Ranga, don't make something up,' Pampa warned. 'This is too important.'

'I won't! Remember the man who came to see Appa late last night?'

Pampa nodded. 'He was from the office of Minister Timma.'

'I heard Appa and him talk and he asked the same two questions as Ajji.'

'How could you hear them? Appa closed the door of the living room and told Amma and me to stay away.'

'Right, but not me,' Ranga gave a gap-toothed grin. 'I lost a marble, it had rolled under the divan and I crawled under it to get it. Just then Appa and that man came in, Appa slammed the door and I was stuck. So I stayed very quiet under the divan and I heard everything.' As we leaned forward eagerly, I could see Ranga was having fun. 'That man said that Minister Timma has still not told His Majesty about the theft—but if the necklaces were not found soon, he would have to.'

'What did Appa say?'

'Nothing. He just listened. The man said that Minister Timma wants answers to two questions. Does Appa have the exact date when the necklaces were placed in the treasury? Then since that time, can he give a list of people who have entered the treasury and could have replaced the real with fake necklaces?'

Pampa looked anxious. 'Appa knew that?'

'He did. He said he had also been thinking about it and asked the same questions and then he had checked the treasury register.'

'What's a treasury register?' I asked.

'There are two registers,' Pampa explained. 'One has a list of all the contents of the treasury and in the second one Appa writes down the date when the treasury door is opened and a list of people who had gone inside.'

'So what did Uncle Raghu say?' I turned back to Ranga who was dying to tell his story.

'Appa said that after the ceremony the necklaces remained on the idols of the goddesses for a fortnight. Two guards were placed in their shrines to keep the jewellery safe.'

'Why a fortnight?'

'Because the temple astrologer had to pick an auspicious day on which the jewellery could be placed in the treasury. The necklaces were placed in the treasury on the 10th day of the month of Bhadra.'

'That is roughly two months ago,' Pampa calculated quickly. 'Today is the 5th of Kartik.'

'How many people entered the treasury?' Pampa asked.

'Appa said that he only opened the treasury once after that for his monthly check last month, and with him there was the assistant priest Diwakar and the guard Kartikeyan. Then day before yesterday he went in with the jeweller who polishes all the gold and this man, the moment he picked up the necklaces, knew they were fake ones.'

After lunch we got more news from Appa. Diwakar and Kartikeyan had been questioned by the minister. Their homes had been searched by soldiers and nothing had been found. Both the men said they were innocent and Appa, who had known them for years, just could not believe that they could steal from the temple.

The two necklaces had vanished into thin air.

৵৽৶

Then we saw Amma come hurrying down the lane and ran up to meet her.

'What's the matter? Are you ill?'

'No, I'm not!' she said shortly. 'Where's your Appa? I have news.'

The cooks had gone off after lunch, so Appa served Amma in the kitchen. She ate a handful of rice and pumpkin curry and said, 'The women at the zenana are talking so much that someone has gone and told Queen Tirumale Devi everything.'

'Oh no!' Appa's eyes were wide with worry, 'Has she spoken to His Majesty? Does Krishna Deva Raya know?'

Amma shook her head. 'She called me and wanted to know the truth. So I told her everything. She agreed with me that Raghavendra could not be a thief but that he has not been doing his job properly. Then I persuaded her to wait and let Saluva Timma decide when to inform His Majesty.'

Amma ate some more as we waited holding our breaths, and then said, 'The queen then summoned the jeweller who had discovered the theft. The man said that the fake necklaces were so well made that Raghu could not have spotted the difference. I asked him if he knew of any jeweller in Vijayanagar who made such glass jewellery.' Amma frowned. 'He said something very odd, that the workmanship was not of Vijayanagar. This kind of glass jewel work was done elsewhere.'

'Where?'

'In the cities of Bijapur and Golconda.' We stared at her in shock. These two kingdoms were our enemies, often attacking Vijayanagar. 'So this could be a planned theft by Bijapur to take revenge for their defeat at Raichur. The royal family believes in omens and they may think this will bring them bad luck. As it is Tirumale Devi is anxious about the fact that His Majesty does not have a son and heir...'

Appa sat holding his chin. 'If Raghu loses his job or is sent to prison, do you know what will happen to the inn?'

Amma nodded grimly.

One of the reasons our inn was always full was because of Uncle Raghu. Many visitors came to the temple all the year round—story tellers, gurus, poets, dancers and musicians—and he put them up at our inn. Then during festivals, food was supplied to feed the devotees. The temple was our biggest customer and we would lose a lot of business without his help.

I had to talk to Ajji.

I rattled the abacus. 'What?' she sounded very irritable, and I remembered Ajji's afternoon nap was very important.

'Listen… I have news…'

'I still think it is one of them… Diwakar or Kartikeyan or both together.'

'They did not find anything in their houses.'

'Of course they won't! They are not stupid to hide the necklaces under their mattresses! So keep an eye on them,' her voice faded and she was gone.

Obeying Ajji, we decided to keep an eye on Diwakar the assistant priest and Kartikeyan the guard. Both were at home with two soldiers sitting and yawning at their doors. Neither was allowed into the temple. Diwakar lived close by but Kartikeyan was a poor man and lived at the other end of Hampi village. The Hemakuta Hill stood right next to the temple and to get to his home we would have to walk for a long time along the hill, past the giant image of Ganesh that stood on top.

Then I remembered something Amma said. When she heard that Kartikeyan was a suspect she shook her head. 'He is an old man who has worked in the temple all his life. Why would he steal now? Also, he is a simple man. I can't see him planning something so clever… fake diamonds… then finding a good hiding place…'

Appa nodded, 'I agree, but what about Diwakar?'

I remembered Diwakar's face, the narrow nose and high forehead where he always wore the sandalwood mark of Shiva; a small firm mouth that never smiled and sharp eyes that did not miss anything. When we went to watch the puja he was always there beside Uncle Raghu, helping with the rituals and chanting the mantras, lighting the lamps and waving the incense. He looked like a very religious man. Could such a man steal?

Amma popped a paan into her mouth and chewed thoughtfully. 'He is young and clever, and much smarter than Raghu. He could easily plan something like this. Also remember he is the son of the last head priest. When his father died suddenly, he wasn't pleased that Raghu was chosen instead of him. He said he was a scholar of sacred Sanskrit texts and had been trained by his father in the right rituals.'

'Raghu was the assistant priest and Diwakar was just helping in the Devi Pampa shrine. And Raghu is a scholar too!' Appa protested.

Amma chewed and shrugged, 'We can suspect anyone we like but as long as the necklaces are not found, there is no proof against anyone.'

Pampa and I were not keen but Keshava and Ranga were very enthusiastic about keeping a watch. Soon they were hanging around the gate of Diwakar's house, until the guards shooed them away. So they returned when it was dark and loitered in the back lane where the guards could not see them.

Pampa and I got the whole story the next morning on the way to the river. Ranga was so excited he was nearly dancing down the lane.

'We saw Diwakar sneak out of the house!' he sang out.

'Leave his house?' Pampa stared at her brother. 'How could he? There are guards at the door.'

'Back window! Back window!'

Keshava and Ranga had crept out after dinner and settled down in the back lane when they saw a downstairs window open. A man very carefully clambered out.

'Was it Diwakar?' I asked.

Keshava shrugged, 'It was too dark, the street torches had died down and all we saw was a shadow. The man bent low and slowly crept down the lane…'

'So we hid behind a tree,' Ranga joined in.

'He crossed the road and went behind the inn,' Keshava went on.

'*Our* inn?' I stared at him.

'Yes! We hid around the corner; luckily it was a moonless night. Two men were waiting for him and they began to whisper in a huddle.'

'Couldn't you hear anything?'

The boys shook their heads. 'We were too far away. Just then some people entered the lane from the opposite side and began to walk towards us. The three men quickly moved away and the man we think was Diwakar walked back the way he had come. So we followed and saw him climb back into the house from that open window.'

'Then!' Ranga was so excited he could barely speak. 'We saw the other two men turn and enter the inn!'

'They are right here in our inn!' By then even Keshava was doing a dance. 'We can catch them now.'

'In our inn?' Padma and I were so surprised we stopped walking and stood staring at the boys.

Later, while drying her wet hair Padma asked, 'What do we do next?'

I was trying to remember the guests in the inn. We had ten rooms, four rooms on the ground floor and six on the first floor. A nobleman and his large family had booked all six rooms on the first floor. On the ground floor the two sari merchants from Kanchipuram had one room; a singer performing at the palace and her daughter had the second room; the third room was empty and in the fourth room there were two men who said they were from Annamalai and had come to buy brassware.

'Two rooms have two men in them.' I turned to the boys. 'You couldn't see their faces?' They shook their heads. My brain was clicking away. 'The men from Kanchipuram have been here for a long time and they could have met Diwakar easily before the theft was discovered but the men from Annamalai came yesterday.'

'Oh I remembered something!' Keshava sat up. 'I served them dinner and they spoke Kannada with a strange accent. As if it was not their mother tongue. One man couldn't remember that our salad is called kosambri and kept saying "I want mixed raw vegetables" until I guessed what he meant.'

'We have to check them out,' Pampa got up. 'Time is running out.'

I had to ask, 'Do we tell Uncle Raghu what the boys saw?'

The others immediately shook their heads.

'Oh no!' Pampa added. 'Appa and Amma are in such a bad mood they would snap my head off.'

'They wouldn't believe us anyway,' Keshava agreed. 'Whoever believes what children tell them?'

'Amma will say I am making it up,' Ranga gave a gloomy shake of his tousled head.

'Well you do imagine things,' Pampa pointed out. 'Remember the story you told of meeting a tiger behind the Hemakuta Hill?'

Ranga just shrugged and then added, 'Appa is hardly home anyway. He is always at the temple.'

'Why?' I asked.

'They are checking everything in the treasury,' Pampa explained. 'Appa, the jeweller and a man from

Minister Timma's office are opening every box and checking everything—jewellery, gold coins, silver utensils, gold and silver images… So Appa eats and sleeps at the temple.'

'Have they found anything else missing?'

Pampa shook her head.

We decided that we would watch the traders from Annamalai for the rest of the day and then report everything to Amma when she came back from the zenana in the afternoon.

'She would know what to do,' I said.

Keshava nodded in agreement, 'Appa will just get excited and upset and flap about. He is useless in a crisis.' Then he nodded thoughtfully, 'I have a plan…'

Whenever we get guests, I have to take down their name and address in the register as the royal officers come to check about guests. Also Appa always chats when he welcomes new guests. So I knew the two men were called Vishnu Chettiar and Shiva Raman and they had given the address of a shop in the main market of Annamalai. It was not suspicious at all as most of our guests were either pilgrims or traders.

An hour later Keshava stood outside their door holding a broom and a wet mop in a pot of water. 'Sir!' he knocked. 'Can I come and clean the room please?'

A sleepy Shiva Raman opened the door and let him in. Standing at the end of the corridor, busily dusting a perfectly clean shelf, I watched him go in. It was a while before he came out and we hurried into the office and closed the door. As Keshava dropped the broom and the mop in a corner, I clacked the abacus beads and then asked breathlessly, 'Did you hear anything?'

'I'm sure they are not from Annamalai because then they should have been speaking in Tamil. They were speaking in Telugu and I couldn't understand everything but I heard the word "Golconda" and also "Nawab".'

Ajji spoke, 'The city of Golconda is the capital of the Bahmani nawabs. They have diamond mines there.'

'Also rubies?'

'Nah! Rubies come from another land across the seas. That is why they are so expensive. They cost more than diamonds.' She would know, she paid all the jewellery bills of the queens and princesses.

'Oh I nearly forgot! I found this under the bed.' Keshava pulled out a sheet of crumpled paper from his pocket. I laid it out on the divan and as we bent over it I felt the soft Ajji style breeze around my right ear.

'Are you reading over my shoulders, Ajji?'

'How else will I know what's written there?'

The words scrawled on the paper were a mix of words and numbers:

On the top it said, 'Garlands of roses and jasmines.'

'4 big roses + 12 small roses + 24 jasmines x 2.
200 x 4 = 800
150 x 12 = 1800
75 x 24 = 1800
4400 x 2 = 8800'

'Ah!' said Ajji quietly into my ear, 'Nice!'

'You know what this means?'

'No. But the calculations are done correctly.'

'How does it help if we don't know what it means, Ajji? What is it? The price of flowers?' I was still staring at the words and suddenly it popped into my mind. 'Of course! It means jewels! White jasmines are diamonds and roses are red rubies!'

'Looks like you do have brains, Durga.'

'So this is the value of the necklaces. Each big ruby is worth 200 gold pana coins and each necklace is worth 4400 gold panas and then multiplied by two…' I stared at the total at the bottom. 'Eight thousand eight hundred gold panas! That is a *lot* of money!'

Keshava shook his head in wonder. 'I have never even seen a gold pana coin!'

'Why do you think they stole it?' Ajji had the last word.

❧

The two men remained inside their room and Keshava and I could not think of another excuse for him to go in. Then in the middle of the morning they came out, entered the food shop and sat down. Keshava promptly slapped a duster on his shoulder and walked up to their table to take their orders. He told them that lunch will only be served after noon but they could get snacks and light drinks.

He came back and yelled at the kitchen door, 'Two plates of idlis with chutney, two vadas, curd and milk drinks, sweet!'

'Serve very slowly.'

'Of course!'

Usually Keshava can carry up to three plates in one go, but today first the glasses of water were taken, then the plates, followed by the idlis and chutney, then the vadas. Watching from my corner I noticed that the men were pretty silent, just eating away. Shiva Raman looked quite unhappy.

Keshava came back. 'Anything?'

'Not much. I heard Vishnu Chettiar say, "It will take longer. We have to wait." They are arguing about something but they would fall silent when I was nearby.'

'I think Diwakar can't get the necklaces from wherever he has hidden them. So they have to wait. And that's making them angry.'

Keshava nodded, 'Oh I remembered something. This morning when I was leaving their room I heard Shiva Raman say something about "It's become dangerous because of the soldiers." Then Chettiar pointed to me and they fell silent.'

No sweets were ordered and the exact change for the bill was given, so Keshava could not hover over their table any more. As we watched, the two men left the inn.

Keshava turned to me. 'What do we do now?'

'Not many customers till lunchtime. Appa can manage. Let's go!'

We slid out of the inn and began to follow Chettiar and Raman. Luckily they were walking very slowly, strolling along like sightseers, clearly in no hurry. They turned into the main avenue of Hampi Bazaar, crowded and busy, as it was the greatest market place not just in Vijayanagar but in any other neighbouring kingdom.

The bazaar had the Virupaksha Temple at one end and the Matanga Hill on the other. On both sides were the stone-pillared shops filled with goods and busy with customers. The doors of the cloth shops were hung with bright saris and angavastrams floating in the breeze; the pottery shop had teetering piles of pots, jars, cooking bowls and plates; at the leather shop shoes and slippers tempted passersby. A rich man got off his horse and entered a food shop; a woman clad in silks and jewels stepped out of a palanquin with her companion, and was welcomed by a jeweller into his shop.

As always the road was full of traffic, people walking, bullock cart drivers yelling at people to move away, palanquins jostling with horses. The two men stopped at a paan shop where the woman paan seller smiled and chatted as she folded the spices into the betel leaf. Right next to her was a flower shop, also run by a woman, with garlands of roses, jasmines and marigolds swaying and filling the air with fragrance. Looking at the flowers I remembered the 'garlands' mentioned on that piece of paper.

Both Keshava and I noticed that the men had gone past three shops selling copper and brassware but did not enter any of them. They did not even slow down to look at the metal utensils.

'Looks like they are not interested in brassware,' Keshava commented.

'Of course they are not! They don't have any shop in Annamalai.'

I looked up as the sun was nearly on top of us. 'It's nearly noon, we'd better go back before Appa starts looking for us.'

As we ran into the food shop, Appa glared at us from the kitchen door. 'Where have you two been? The customers will start coming in any moment now. Get to work!'

Quickly we laid down the cushioned seats on the floor before the low tables. Then for the next couple of hours there was no time to think or plan anything. Keshava and the other two waiters whirled around serving the customers and yelling orders at the cooks sweating over the hot ovens as I scribbled, added and counted the coins.

Late in the afternoon, as Keshava, Appa and I finally sat down to lunch, I decided it was time to tell Appa everything. We told him of the man who climbed out of a window of Diwakar's house and the two men waiting for him who were staying at the inn. Keshava took out the piece of paper and explained how it could be about the necklaces.

Appa sat listening, forgetting to eat and then staring at us in astonishment. 'You four worked all this out by yourself?'

'With some help from Ajji,' I thought happily.

Appa got up. 'Keshava, go and fetch Raghu.' He turned to me. 'You go to the zenana and tell your Amma everything.'

Keshava and Ranga headed for the temple as Pampa and I began a long trek to the zenana. Amma had a royal palanquin, we did not.

We took the road connecting Hampi Bazaar to the royal citadel where all the palaces stood. On the right were the tall wood and stone palaces of the king and the offices of his ministers. On the left, behind high stone walls, was the quarters of the royal women, called the zenana. Along the way there were temples, horse and elephant stables, soldiers' quarters, offices—

it was all very confusing and I had to keep asking people for directions.

At the gate of the zenana a guard stopped us, lowering his moustached face to glare at us. 'And where do you think you two are going?'

I swallowed, 'I have to see my Amma, she works here. It is very important, Sir!'

He crossed his arms, a glimmer of a smile curving his lips, 'And who is your Amma?'

'Parvati Ammal, she is the accountant in the zenana,' and then I added desperately, 'I'm Sundari Ammal's granddaughter Durga. Please can we go in?'

With a grand wave the guard let us in. I heard Pampa give a small sigh of relief.

We entered a women's world and got lost again. There were so many halls, pavilions, lotus pools, gardens. In front was the palace called Lotus Mahal with its pretty fluted pillars and arches where the senior queens lived. Amma had shown it to me the last time I had come here. There were women everywhere—maids carrying baskets of flowers or clothes; princesses swimming in the lotus pools and children playing in the garden… how was I going to find Amma here? I was about to ask a maid when I heard Amma's voice.

'Durga! Pampa!' Amma was hurrying towards us, 'What's the matter? Why are you two here?'

'You have to come with us. It's about the necklaces…' Pampa said urgently.

'Wait!' Amma went back into a room and came out immediately. 'Let's go! We'll take my palanquin.'

Pampa and I exchanged happy glances. No more walking. What a relief!

Pampa, Ranga, Keshava and I sat with our parents as we planned what to do next. Appa wanted to call the soldiers immediately but Amma shook her head.

'There is no proof except the word of four children and they belong to our families. Diwakar will say we have taught them to say this. No one will believe us and Diwakar is a powerful man. Unless we can catch the men with the necklaces we have nothing that can't be denied. That piece of paper could mean anything. I know Minister Timma, he has a suspicious mind and will be very hard to convince.'

Uncle Raghu nodded. 'But how do we find the necklaces? Diwakar has been questioned and even threatened with punishment but he is not talking.'

Pampa's mother, who had been listening quietly, spoke, 'The two men are waiting and getting impatient. So Diwakar has to recover the necklaces quickly from wherever he has hidden them. That's when we have to catch him. He can't wait too long because Chettiar and Raman could just as easily go away.'

The plan was that Keshava and Ranga would keep

watch in the lane and Appa and Uncle Raghu would wait behind the inn and wait for Diwakar to act. The girls and women would have to stay at home. It did not make Pampa or me very happy.

When Keshava and Ranga came back, the sky was beginning to go light and they entered the inn with huge grins on their faces. Ranga was dancing again.

Later Keshava and I told Ajji of their adventures.

'Just like the night before, Ajji,' Keshava said, 'Diwakar climbed out of the window and we were ready for him!'

'Stop your drama and tell me what happened,' Ajji said impatiently.

'As Appa and Uncle Raghu watched from the shadows, Diwakar met Chettiar and Raman in the lane behind the inn and then they began to walk.'

'Where?'

'To the temple tank!'

'Ahh! Of course. He hid it in the water. Very clever!'

'Diwakar ran down the steps and slipped into the water and began to search and soon came up carrying a cloth bundle. That was when Appa and Uncle Raghu ran up waving sticks. Ranga and I began calling the guards from the temple who came immediately and caught the men.'

'Oh good!' Ajji gave a happy sigh.

I laughed, 'His story is not over yet.'

'Two men were holding down Diwakar who was kicking and punching, then one guard let go of his legs to grab the bundle that he was holding. Diwakar was all wet and slippery and he slid out of their grip and began to run! That's when I dived and caught hold of his ankle and he went crashing down.'

'Oh Shiva! You were so brave!' Ajji's voice was full of admiration. 'I have such clever grandchildren. I am so proud of you, Keshava and Durga.'

'Minister Saluva Timma questioned Diwakar and the two men,' I continued with the story. 'They were not from Annamalai at all and their names are not Vishnu Chettiar and Shiva Raman. They are diamond merchants from Golconda who had supplied the stones from the diamond mines there to the Vijayanagar jewellers who made the necklaces. At that time they had met Diwakar and the three of them hatched a plot.'

'Why did Diwakar do this?'

'Diwakar wanted to become the head priest and it was revenge at Raghu Uncle. A few weeks after the victory ceremony, the men came back with the necklaces set with fake diamonds that they had got made at Golconda. Diwakar exchanged them when he and Uncle Raghu went in for their monthly check.'

'What Diwakar did not expect was that the temple jeweller would spot the fake necklaces so quickly,' Keshava added.

'By the time the two men arrived from Golconda, Diwakar was being guarded at home and couldn't get the necklaces that were hidden in the temple tank. He crept out at night and met the men but he got scared as people came into the lane. Then on the second night he took out the bag with the necklaces from the water.'

Late that night, after all the excitement had died down and everyone was asleep, I lit a lamp and went into the office again to touch the abacus beads.

'Ajji, you there?'

'Yes I am, Durga.'

'You know, we couldn't have done it without you. You are so clever. You saved Uncle Raghu and his family.'

'Not true! You four children did it by your own cleverness and you were brave. These men were criminals and they could have hurt you. I was there to guide you, that is all.' The soft breeze around my face was like a warm embrace. 'And one day Durga, I know that you will take over from your mother at the zenana. I am sure of that. Then when you step out of the palanquin at the gate, the guards will bow and say, "Namaskara Durgamma, and how are you today?"'

I laughed a little shakily, my eyes flooding with tears. Then I realized how quiet and empty the room felt.

Ajji was gone.

KiTE-FLYiNG DAYS

'What do you think?' Dhani asked with a frown. 'Sky is clear,' brooded Shahid, hand on his hips, thoughtfully studying the sky. 'No dark clouds,' sounding exactly like a solemn weatherman on television, 'so no chance of rain… good breeze…'

'Oh stop fussing!' Padma gave a happy sigh. 'Let's go! It's the perfect day for flying kites.'

They were standing on the third-floor terrace of Shahid's house. It was a monsoon afternoon in August and the sky had finally cleared after two days of continuous rain. Having to stay indoors all day had made them go a bit crazy. What was the point of playing board games and watching television when they could fly kites?

Dhani, who was still studying the sky, gave a dreamy smile. 'Just perfect.'

A few cotton wool clouds floated high in the deep blue sky like castles from fairy tales. The breeze was blowing in gentle gusts through the trees in the park and would make their kite soar like an eagle.

Padma, Dhani and Shahid were the champion kite-flying team of their lane in Delhi's Chandni Chowk. Flying kites also meant a running battle with the kite fliers of all the galis. Already there were colourful squares of paper floating in the blue sky, and it was kite cutting time! This was a serious sport and it took a lot of practice. They needed skill to fly their kite the highest and then make it dip and cut the string of the other kite.

Soon they were back on the terrace with the kites they had bought from Old Fakru's kite shop in Ballimaran. Everyone knew that Fakru's kites were expensive but they were also the best in the Old City. They loved wandering around his tiny shop where the walls and doors were covered with multicoloured kites—big and small kites, some with faces on them, others with long tails... Fakru sat in one corner slicing thin bamboo sticks, cutting the paper and mixing the glue. As Dhani said admiringly, Old Fakru was a paper artist.

Padma bought a black and red kite with a long tail. Dhani's choice was a kite in stripes of saffron, white and green—the colours of the Indian flag—because he planned to fly it on 15th August, India's Independence Day. In Delhi, everyone flew kites on that day. Shahid's kite had two black eyes painted on the yellow paper that made it look like a dangerous monster. They had also bought two rolls of kite string, tightly wound around wooden spindles. Fakru's kite string was sharp and tough and it was the secret weapon of their kite battles. You had to handle the string very carefully because if you were careless it could cut your fingers.

'Ready, Padma?' asked Shahid, holding up the black and red kite; Padma gripped the string and nodded, ready to pull; Dhani stood behind her with the reel of string. Once the kite was in the air, they would take turns flying it.

Shahid jumped, throwing up the kite as high as he could go. At the same time, Padma gave a sharp pull and then let the string go, letting the kite catch a patch of breeze so that it began to soar. Pulling and letting go…pulling and letting go… soon the kite was floating high, its long tail trailing behind it like a flying snake.

Dhani looked around. On every terrace there were people flying kites and the sky was filled with bright squares in every colour of a paint box—blue and green; red and yellow; black and purple…

'It's like a painting,' he said dreamily, 'a huge painting of a smiling sky.'

Shahid, who was now flying the kite, grinned at him. 'Dhani our poet.'

'Imagine thinking kites make the sky smile!' Padma laughed.

They had become distracted talking and did not see the green and yellow kite that came swooping towards their kite from a hidden corner of the sky. Like a hungry falcon it twirled around their string, a sharp pull—and snap! As they watched in horror, the red and black square began a sad, swaying descent towards the ground.

'Ohh nooo…' Padma breathed sadly.

In a flash they were clambering down the stairs, all ready to rescue their kite.

'It was going towards the back lane!' Shahid yelled.

Huffing and puffing, they ran to the back lane, turned a corner, their heads raised to the sky, eyes firmly on the floating red and black square. 'There it is!' Padma pointed as it vanished behind a house. It was hard rescuing a kite in that crowded gali. They swerved around people and cycle rickshaws; avoided crashing into bicycles, carts and cows….

'It's going down!' Dhani panted desperately.

'Oh!'

The kite had vanished.

They came to a panting stop at the end of the lane that ended in houses in a blocked corner. Here it was suddenly very quiet as there were no shops or traffic, just a spreading banyan tree and the walls and windows of houses.

Where did the kite go? They looked around.

'I think I saw it go there,' Dhani pointed to a high wall with a small door in the middle, that stood right at the end of the lane in the shadow of the banyan tree.

The door had a thick iron chain hanging from the top and Padma began to rattle it vigorously. 'Oye, open the door!' and then she asked, 'Who lives in this haveli?'

Shahid grinned. 'The two women you're so scared of—Banno Bi and her granddaughter.'

'Oh!' Padma promptly lowered her hand. 'I'd forgotten they lived here.'

They knew most of the people who lived in their gali and they were welcome in their houses, except for this one where people only went for special reasons. You did not drop in for a cup of tea and a chat, you only knocked on this door if you were ill and needed medicines for coughs and fevers; or you wanted magic spells to make a man fall in love with you; or order nasty potions to curse an enemy. They knew very well that kids did not run into Banno Bi's courtyard after a kite. It could be very dangerous to do so. You never knew what she would do.

Banno Bi was easy to spot when she walked down the gali. She was always clad in a snowy white kurta and loose salwars, her feet shod in flappy embroidered mojri chappals and over her head she would sweep up a huge white dupatta. Sometimes her dupatta would slip off her head and reveal hair dyed with henna in a bright orange that gleamed so much you could spot it from across the road and think, 'Ah! There goes Banno Bi to buy vegetables and fight with the sabziwala over the price of onions.' Everyone knew that she liked to fight.

In their young eyes, Banno Bi looked very old. The fair, sharp-featured face was lined with fine wrinkles; the big droopy dark eyes were thickly lined with kajal and the thin lips reddened with paan. She would stroll down the gali as if she owned it, pausing to chat with the shopkeepers, greeting the people like a queen. Then she would pause at a corner and spit paan juice against a wall and no one had the courage to protest. Who could risk being cursed by her?

'The old witch lives here,' Shahid gave a small smile. 'Want to go in and ask her for your kite?'

Suddenly, with a rattle and squeak, the bolt was pulled away from inside, the door swung open and they were looking at the second-most scary woman of their gali—Tarana Begum, Banno Bi's granddaughter. To make matters worse, she looked like a younger version of her grandmother. Seeing Tarana you knew that at one time Banno Bi must have been very beautiful. Tarana had delicate skin pale as milk, pinkish lips and large dark eyes under curving brows. She wore a small nose ring on the high bridged nose and her dark hair floated around her face in a riot of curls. She was wearing a blue blouse over a wraparound skirt in blue and white and her bare feet, peeping out from under her skirt, had toes painted a pretty pink.

So it was a bit odd that this beautiful young woman had a biri clenched in her teeth as she gave them an irritated look.

'You can't wear a wraparound skirt from Sarojini Nagar and be a witch,' Padma thought, feeling a bit puzzled. 'Not done.'

'Kya?' she looked at them with a mighty frown from behind the biri smoke. The large eyes surveyed their faces and she clearly did not like what she saw. 'We don't give medicines to children. Tell your parents to come.'

Dhani frowned back, 'Medicine? Who wants medicine?'

Tarana dropped the butt of the biri on the ground and studied the three children standing at her door. Something about them had got her interested. 'Then why were you knocking?'

'My kite,' Padma waved at the courtyard behind Tarana. 'It got cut and has fallen into your courtyard… there…'

'Can we get it please?' Shahid gave his best begging look. 'Won't take a minute. It cost seventy rupees and if we lose it Padma's Amma will kill her.'

Tarana gave a slight smile and then stood back to let them in. 'Be quick. I'm working, so don't disturb me.'

They entered the courtyard shaded by mango trees and with many kinds of vegetables and herbs growing in neat rows below them. They spotted coriander and mint, peas and tiny tomatoes. Dhani looked around and to his relief Banno Bi was nowhere in sight. Her glare could make Dhani go weak in the knees and make him want to run and hide. Up close, Tarana did not seem as scary as her but the important question was, could a witch's granddaughter be as dangerous as a grandmother witch?

It was a very old haveli with dark rooms behind a veranda and Tarana had disappeared into the corner room. A snow white cat with grey eyes sat on top of a broken garden wall studying them. Then they spotted the kite hanging forlornly by the string from a branch of the mango tree. As Dhani gave him a leg up, Shahid hauled himself up the tree and began to climb.

'As good as a monkey!' Padma grinned.

'Monkeys get the fruit,' Shahid yelled and from somewhere inside Tarana yelled back, 'Don't you dare touch my mangoes!'

'Yes, Ma'am,' said Shahid, clambering down with the kite.

They stood at the door of the room where Tarana was working. Shahid wondered what they could call the large space. There were a gas stove, a mixer-grinder and a fridge, cooking pots and pans, a toaster, plates and bowls, masala bottles and vegetables in baskets, so it was a kitchen. However, on one side there was a long marble-topped table on which stood a big iron mortar and pestle, a grinding stone and a row of glass jars, some looking like test tubes and pipettes, pretty similar to the equipment in their school chemistry laboratory. There was a large wooden chopping board and a stand with knives and various kinds of wooden spoons. Behind the table there was a shelf with rows of glass bottles with labels on them in Urdu. They did not look like the masalas you would use in cooking.

'What is this strange place?' Shahid wondered to himself, 'A kitchen-lab?'

Tarana was working at the marble-topped table, mashing herbs on the grinding stone. She looked up. 'Found it?'

'Yes. Thank you,' Padma dipped her head. 'We're sorry we disturbed you.'

'Not a problem. Sometimes I get bored with all this grinding... mixing...' Tarana was rolling the stone, 'but Dadi won't let me use a mixie. Not for her herbal mixtures. What can I do?'

'That is a good idea. You could just pop in the herbs in the mixie and whizz,' Dhani said.

'Exactly!'

'I didn't know that wit... I mean doctors,' Shahid stumbled on, 'use mixies.'

'I'm not a doctor. I'm a naturopath.' She gave him a sharp look, 'You were about to say "witch", weren't you?'

'Err... not really...' Shahid blinked nervously.

'I am a witch, just like my Dadi. We are white hat witches.'

By then they were gathered around the table, 'White what?'

'White hat. We are good witches who help people. The black hats are the nasty ones, who curse and put spells on people.' Tarana began to spoon up the paste into a plastic jar. 'I saw a programme on YouTube about white and black hat witches and I knew immediately what I was.'

'You watch YouTube?!' they stared at her in amazement.

'Of course! On my smartphone. I also have a website. Check out www.naturewitch.com. I get lots of hits from people looking for natural remedies.' Then she laughed at their astonished faces. 'I reply to their emails on my laptop.'

Their astonished faces said, 'Smartphone! Website!! White hat witch!!!' and that made Tarana laugh even more.

'Want some mango panna?' she asked and at their eager nod, she poured out three glasses of the cool drink from a jug in the fridge. 'This is from the raw mangoes from that tree you climbed just now.'

'I thought your house would have only really old things,' Padma began, settling comfortably on a mura, 'You know…'

'I know. Huge pots boiling on an open fire; Dadi and me flying around waving ladles, smoke and nasty smells… Right?'

They nodded vigorously.

'That only happens in films. Dadi and I run a business of natural remedies. We make the herbal potions fresh for each customer to match what they need.' She was sounding like an advertisement for naturewitch. 'You think we only treat people from Chandni Chowk? My orders come from all across the country by email, messages and Whatsapp. People discuss their health problems on the phone.'

'Too brilliant!' Padma breathed admiringly.

'Now go home,' Tarana said briskly. 'I have work to do.'

Monsoon days are special in Chandni Chowk. After the long, hot and dusty months of summer the rains wash everything clean. The leaves on the trees turn a shining green and sparkle in the mellow sunlight and the air smells of wet earth. In the morning when they wake up, the sound of the azaan, the call to prayer rises from the mosque and blends with the rush of a shower.

Then when they head out to school, the shabad kirtan hymns sing out from the gurdwara and as they wander along, jumping over puddles, the bells begin to ring in the temples. Dhani calls it monsoon music and as he never remembers to bring his own, he huddles under his friends' umbrellas. Going past the sweet shop in the corner they happily sniff at the smell of ghee as the mithaiwalla makes the special monsoon sweets called ghewar and pheni. Even going to school becomes interesting on rainy days.

Next morning, they were still talking about Tarana, the naturewitch.

'I asked Ammi about her and Banno Bi,' Shahid began, 'she said that the haveli has been in Banno Bi's family for many generations. She began to treat sick people and sell herbal medicines after her husband died. She had a young daughter…'

'Tarana's mother.'

'Right. The daughter died when Tarana was very young and her father just walked away and got married again. So Banno Bi brought up Tarana and taught her the Unani medical system and now Tarana runs the business.'

'She smoked biris,' Padma still could not get over the sight of the young woman. 'I find that so strange.'

'Unani medicines are fine,' Dhani asked the crucial questions. 'But are they witches as everyone says?'

'Ammi says that she has no idea and doesn't care. Witches are all fairy tales anyway. All she knows is that Banno Bi makes the best medicines for stomach aches, fevers, coughs and toothache.'

'So white hat witches,' Padma had the last word.

That evening Dhani asked, 'Kites or the swing?'

'Swing!' said the other two.

There was a peepal tree in Padma's courtyard where her father had tied a swing. They had the usual fight about who would go first. When it was Padma's turn, she stood on the swing as Shahid pushed and she bent her knee and pushed, going higher and higher until she was soaring so high she could look over the courtyard wall.

Watching her rise high Dhani wondered, 'Suppose she lets go of the rope, what will happen, do you think?'

'She'll go flying in the air and land in Daryagunj,' Shahid grinned. 'Padma the astronaut.'

They laughed aloud and then realized that Padma had not joined in. Instead she was slowing down the swing and then as it came to a stop she hopped off and said, 'I saw something really strange just now.' She waved to the next door house. 'You know that old lady who lives there?'

Dhani nodded. 'Papa calls her Gul Chachi.'

'You know, going up I could see into her house and she was standing on the upstairs veranda and waving and calling out to someone in the lane. Then the swing came down and I couldn't see who. When I rose again Chachi was being dragged inside by her daughter-in-law and she was crying really loudly.'

'Crying?' Shahid turned to the courtyard door, 'Let's go and check. Why should an old lady be crying?'

As they walked down the lane, Dhani asked Padma, 'Do you know the family?'

'Not really. Amma sometimes goes across to chat with Chachi. To give her Diwali sweets or get a recipe, because Chachi is a good cook. I have never been inside the house.'

'What about the daughter-in-law?'

'Amma doesn't like her.'

The courtyard door was open and they walked across the front garden but the main door of the house was closed and Dhani pressed the calling bell. The door was flung open and the grim-faced daughter-in-law stood glaring at them.

'What do you want?' she snapped.

Padma swallowed nervously and thought quickly, 'Err... Aunty... my mother sent me,' she waved towards her home. 'We live next door? My Amma said that Chachiji was going to give her some recipes...'

'Not now! She is not well. Come next week.' And bang! the door was slammed shut on their faces.

'What was that?' Walking back they stared at each other.

'Do you think we should tell someone?' Padma asked anxiously.

'Nah! People fight.' Dhani gave a gusty sigh. 'You should see my Amma and Didi, arguing all the time.' And he mimicked his mother, '"You will not go to the movies! Good girls don't wear trousers! Switch off that phone!" Nag... nag... One day, I'm telling you, Didi will just walk out of the house and not come back.'

Dhani and Shahid did not seem to be very worried but Padma could not forget Chachi's tearful face. Her Amma described Gul Chachi as a kind and gentle person and anyone bullying gentle people made Padma hopping mad. Maybe Dhani was right and it was just a fight? Still, Padma could not forget.

Next afternoon, she had gone to the stationery shop to get a box of colour pencils for an art project when she spotted a familiar figure across the road. It was Tarana and today she was wearing a yellow t-shirt and loose black trousers, her curly hair tied in a pony tail. She was buying mangoes from a fruit cart.

Padma strolled across the road, crept up very quietly behind Tarana and said suddenly, 'Hello, Tarana Didi!'

'Oh!' Tarana jumped and turned to look at her. 'It's you! Padma, isn't it?'

Padma nodded, oddly happy to see her.

The fruit seller weighing the mangoes asked, 'How about some plums?'

'Next time. And how is your son?'

'The fever is gone, Begum, and he's playing around the house again,' the man smiled gratefully at Tarana.

'Good. Come in the evening and I'll give you a potion to build his energy.'

Padma carried the bag of litchis as they walked companionably down the lane. 'Do you know that some people in the gali are scared of your grandmother?'

Tarana gave a short laugh, 'I don't blame them. I am scared of her sometimes.'

'She is also umm... a white hat?'

Tarana frowned, 'I'm not too sure. Dadi likes to curse and she loses her temper very quickly. Though... I don't know if she would put a bad spell on anyone.'

'She knows bad spells?' Padma asked in fright.

'Quite a few. Spells to make people's stomach ache or make the walls of their houses shake; send in djinns to create trouble...'

'What's a djinn?'

'Djinns are spirits that obey her,' said Tarana. *She spoke so casually, as if she was discussing the weather or something,* thought Padma. Tarana brooded for a while and then said thoughtfully, 'At least she says she can do that... call a djinn. I think she is not black or white, but sort of grey...'

'Do you put spells too?'

Tarana shook her head. 'I am a naturopath. I like helping people.'

Later Padma never knew what made her say, 'Then maybe you can help Gul Chachi. I think she's in trouble but Shahid and Dhani don't take me seriously.'

'Gul Chachi? What's happened to her?'

'She lives next door.'

'I know.'

'Yesterday I was on the swing and going really high so that I could see into their courtyard. Chachi was standing upstairs and waving and calling to someone in the lane. Then I saw her daughter-in-law drag her inside and Chachi did not want to go and she was crying loudly…'

'Crying?' Tarana stood stock still, looking worried, 'I have to tell Dadi. She comes to Dadi for medicines and they are old friends.' She began to hurry home and then turned to Padma, 'Will you come and describe what you saw?'

Padma gave a nervous laugh. 'Talk to Banno Bi?'

Tarana grinned, 'I'll hold your hand. She's just an old woman, Padma.'

Banno Bi was sitting propped up with pillows in an old four poster bed, a pair of round spectacles perched at the end of her nose, reading an Urdu newspaper. Her snow white cat sat leaning against her leg; he raised his head and studied them with cool grey eyes.

Banno Bi looked at them over her glasses and said, 'That took you a long time.'

Tarana dumped the bags of fruit on a table, 'Dussehri mangoes as you ordered. Want some aam panna?'

Banno Bi had spotted Padma hovering behind Tarana, 'And who is that?'

'This is Padma, she flies kites and has something to tell you.'

'She looks scared.' The old woman gave an oddly cold grin, showing red paan-stained teeth. 'I won't eat you, child. Come closer.'

'You can scare policemen, this is just a small girl.' Tarana said briskly. 'Be nice to her, Dadi, please. This is important. I think Gul Chachi is in trouble because Padma saw something.'

'Gulbadan? What's happened to her?' Banno Bi folded and put away the newspaper, took off her glasses and said surprisingly gently, 'Sit here and tell me everything.'

Sipping the aam panna, Padma told her story again and the old lady listened patiently. Sitting near her, Padma realized that Banno Bi wasn't so scary after all, she was just another old woman with red teeth. She spoke as Padma ended her tale.

'I knew this would happen. I told Gul not to let that boy into her house! But will she listen to me? Of course not! All overflowing with motherly love... hah!'

'What boy?' Tarana and Padma asked together.

'Gul was very young when her husband died and she had no children. So she adopted her brother's son and brought the boy home. They were very well off and she spoilt that child rotten, sent him to an expensive school, then college and then got him married last year. Now she complains that he is lazy and not looking for any work and spending her money buying expensive things for his wife. If only she had listened to me...'

'You saw something in the baby?' Tarana said.

Padma wondered, what can you possibly see in a baby? They all look the same, all scrunched up faces, crying and pooping all the time.

'I did. When Gul brought the child home he was a month old and she called me to say the prayers and take away the nazar,' she glanced at Padma's puzzled face, 'you know, against the evil eye...'

Padma nodded, 'Good spells to fight bad spells?'

'Right. I went and touched the child's head and I knew!'

'How?' Padma was puzzled again.

'A touch can tell you a lot,' Tarana explained. 'We can often feel trouble or even smell or taste it in the air.'

'He did not smell right either,' Banno Bi nodded. 'There was a bitter smell, like burning paper...'

'From a *little baby*?' Padma had enough of the mumbo jumbo and had to protest. 'Oh come on!

Babies smell of talcum powder, my cousin sister's just had one.'

Banno Bi turned her head very, very slowly and stared at her and suddenly Padma's heart began to thud. The eyes had turned into glittering slits, the eyelids drooping in a sinister way like an angry cat. Then she reached out a thin, long-fingered hand and touched Padma on the forehead, and on a sweaty monsoon day Padma suddenly felt shivery and cold.

'When I talk little girrrll, you lisssten…'

'Yes ma'am!' said Padma very obediently and Tarana laughed.

'When Gulbadan got the boy married last year, again I told her that the girl was not right for him but again she wouldn't listen. That girl is the daughter of Dilbar Khan and he is a crook, but who was listening to me?'

'What are the son and daughter-in-law called?' Tarana asked suddenly.

'Barkat Ali and Tabassum,' Banno Bi looked thoughtfully at her granddaughter. 'Will you do it or do I have to get out of bed?'

'Do what?' Padma's head was swivelling back and forth, her mouth open in surprise and then she began to get excited. 'Curses? Magic spells? Ohhh… djinns?'

The two women laughed. Tarana's laughter was a pretty sight, her teeth gleaming between her pink lips.

Banno Bi's red teeth seemed to glitter like the open mouth of a sleepy crocodile.

Oh she is all witchy and djinni, Padma decided, and this is getting very, very interesting.

'I'll need something from the house,' Tarana said thoughtfully. 'I need an excuse to get inside.'

'Gul orders my clove oil and mulethi powder for her toothache. Take some and say she had ordered it.'

'Are you sure, Dadi,' Tarana was still not completely convinced, 'that Tabassum is hurting Gul Chachi? I mean, why would she do that?'

'For the house. Gul does not have much money left and Barkat Ali has to start working but he is not trying at all. He gets jobs, works for a few months and quits, that spoilt and lazy piece of…' and then Padma heard some amazing rude abuses in chaste Urdu. 'Now Tabassum's father Dilbar Khan, who is a property dealer, has put it in their heads that they should make Gul sell the house.'

'Ah!' Tarana's eyebrows danced in amusement, 'It's all about paisa! That makes it all very clear. I'll get to work.'

Padma followed Tarana out of the room, 'So what will I do?'

'Make the tooth powder.'

They were in the kitchen-cum-lab again and Tarana put a bunch of dry herbs in the mortar and pestle and began to pound. Padma sat on a high stool next to the marble-topped table sipping her aam panna. It was afternoon and soon the steady pounding and Tarana humming softly under her breath made her sleepy. Her eyelids began to droop, going slightly out of focus and hazy. She thought she saw Tarana turn away to get something from the shelves behind her but the pestle was still pounding away, going up and down, up and down, like a machine. Padma sat up and blinked and saw that Tarana was holding the pestle just like before.

The room was very quiet except for the thump… thump… rattle… thump… of the pestle and Tarana seemed to become wavy at the edges as if she was moving underwater. Were her fingers getting long and her nails all pointy as she stirred the mixture with her hand? Padma blinked and it was the old Tarana again.

'Can aam panna make you dream with your eyes open?' she wondered sleepily.

'You are sleepy, aren't you?' Tarana asked softly.

'Yesss… a little.'

Tarana was leaning close to her face, 'What do you see, Padma?'

'Your eyes… I thought they were black but now they are green… you look like a cat…' Padma mumbled.

Tarana moved back, looking quite like her old self again, and said briskly, 'You are dreaming. Go home.'

Then as Padma hopped off the stool she added, 'I have a plan. Will you three come here tomorrow after school?'

'Sure. What do you plan to do?'

'I'm going to make an ittar perfume to scare people.'

Padma yawned as she walked away, 'Good idea. See you tomorrow.'

Next afternoon, three excited kids stood expectantly at the haveli door and when Tarana opened the door they noticed that she was dressed in a very traditional witch style—like Banno Bi. She wore a white kurta and churidar pajamas and a blue and pink striped dupatta covering her hair that she had tied in a neat pony tail. There were silver bangles at her wrist and small earrings in her earlobes and for a change, she smelled of perfume instead of biri. She led them to the kitchen lab and they saw that a basket of flowers sat on the marble table, and next to it a tiny cut glass bottle.

Dhani bent and sniffed the flowers; it was a mix of roses, marigolds, jasmines and a bunch of tiny purple flowers he had never seen before.

Today there was a bowl of plums for them and as they chewed Tarana told them her plan.

'I will go in with the tooth powder and ask to see Gul Chachi. Padma will come with me. While I am talking to Gul Chachi—and I'm sure Tabassum will be near us listening because she won't leave Chachi alone with me—Padma will slip away,' and she gave Padma a small paper packet. 'Find the kitchen and mix this powder in the salt jar.'

Padma opened the packet and inside there was greyish powder. She sniffed it but it had no smell.

'Meanwhile you two,' Tarana turned to the boys, 'will wait in the lane and only enter the front garden after we have gone inside. I don't want Tabassum to see you. You have two jobs to do.'

Shahid gave a snarky grin, 'Bury bones in the garden?'

'Leave a headless chicken in the veranda?' Dhani was having fun.

'Don't be ridiculous!' Tarana snapped at them. 'What do you think this is? A horror film?' She picked up a roll of thick red string. 'You'll pick one of the trees and tie this string around the trunk. Run it round as many times as you can.'

'Oooh!' Shahid was still feeling doubtful. 'Magic thread, is it?'

'No. It's embroidery thread from Ajay Stores. I bought it this morning.'

'What else?'

'I'm going to make a flowery ittar perfume and put it in this,' she picked up the small bottle. 'I checked in the morning: Tabassum puts the clothes to dry on a clothes line in the front garden. You will sprinkle some of this ittar on the ladies' kurtas and gents' shirts.'

'Clothes that Barkat Ali and Tabassum wear?' Dhani asked.

'Clever boy. Now finish the plums while I make the ittar.'

Shahid and Dhani were sitting in the veranda but Padma was back on the high stool watching Tarana work. She reached up to a shelf and brought down a different mortar and pestle. This one was small and made of gleaming white marble. The bowl was shaped like a flower with delicate patterns carved on the side.

'Ohh... this is so pretty!'

'This is used only to grind flower petals. Dadi says that this mortar and pestle belonged to Nurjahan Begum's mother.' Tarana was pouring handfuls of petals into the bowl. 'Her name was Asmat Begum.'

'Nurjahan? You mean the Mughal queen?'

'Who else? Asmat Begum created the ittar of roses and Emperor Jahangir was so pleased he presented her with a pearl necklace.'

Padma gently touched the bowl, the marble cool under her fingers. 'Where did your grandmother find it?'

'She says her grandmother's grandmother... or something like that... used to work for Asmat Begum in Agra and she kept the bowl when her mistress died.'

'Wow!' Padma breathed, trying to remember the dates of Nurjahan and failing completely, so she said lamely, 'It's hundreds of years old...'

Beginning to grind, Tarana shook her head. 'Maybe and maybe not. Dadi has a vivid imagination. You shouldn't believe everything she says. I've seen bowls like this at the Kinari Bazaar shops.'

'Still, it is a lovely story.'

'So it is.'

Padma was feeling sleepy and dreamy again and her eyelids began to droop. She laid her head on her arms and looked absently at the basket of flowers. Why were the tiny purple flowers floating up and hovering in the air like purple butterflies? She shut her eyes and opened them and they were back in the basket again. Tarana seemed to be reciting something softly under her breath in a sing-song beat. Padma closed her eyes and listened to the gentle, soothing song.

Next when she looked up, Tarana was putting the mashed-up petals in a small glass bowl and adding oil, then she began to mix it vigorously with a large spoon. She was still singing away and it seemed as if a thin stream of smoke was flowing out of her mouth but Padma could not smell any biri. All she could smell was the fragrance of flowers. Tarana was busy putting away the vials of oils on the shelves with her back to the table but the spoon was still stirring away, making a noisy rattle. Padma closed her eyes and her nap was perfumed by roses and jasmines.

'Sleep, Padma...' Tarana was singing softly in her

ear, 'sleeeep till I wake you…' and Padma was out like a light.

A gentle shake of her shoulders and Padma sat up feeling surprisingly refreshed as Tarana yelled, 'Boys! Come and get the ittar.'

Shahid stared at the ittar bottle, shook the pale liquid inside and asked doubtfully, 'What can this possibly do?'

'Send a djinn into their house,' said a voice behind them, and they turned to see Banno Bi standing at the door fanning herself with a hand fan.

'A djinn that will scare them till they come begging to my door.'

'Stop scaring them, Dadi,' Tarana said firmly. Then she waved at them, 'Let's go! And don't forget what I told you to do.'

Along the way, Tarana said to Padma, 'After you have mixed the powder in the salt, on your way back try to pick up something. I want something that they use.'

'Spoons?' Padma asked puzzled, 'Masala?'

'No… no… not from the kitchen. Something from Tabassum's bedroom would be good but if you can't get it, that is okay. I can manage.'

'Who gets scared by red string and flower ittar…' Shahid was still playing the mad scientist.

'One more comment like that, my friend,' Tarana snapped, 'and you are going home.'

'Okay I'll shut up.' Shahid said reluctantly and then added under his breath, 'This is not scientific at all.'

Tarana, who had walked ahead, turned to frown at them. 'What did you say?'

'Nothing!' Shahid kept his head down but Dhani, who was looking at Tarana's face, thought the pupils of her eyes flashed green and then gold like a traffic light—but then they were black again. Just for a second she had looked very dangerous indeed.

The boys hovered anxiously in the lane as Tarana and Padma went through the open door into the front garden. Tarana was about to press the calling bell when the door was flung open and Tabassum stood glaring at them. Padma wondered how a pretty young woman could scowl in such an ugly way.

'Yes?' Padma had never heard an angrier 'Yes' in her life.

'I've come from Banno Bi's dispensary, ma'am,' Tarana was very polite. 'She has sent the medicine that Gul Begum had ordered.'

Tabassum reached out a hand. 'My mother-in-law is not well. Give it to me, I'll give it to her.'

Tarana held on to the jar of tooth powder. 'No ma'am, I have to examine the patient's teeth first. I also have to ask her about her backache; maybe she needs more of the massage oil for the problem.'

Very reluctantly Tabassum let them in and then

looked suspiciously at Padma who had followed them inside. 'Why is this girl with you?'

'She lives next door and I have to see her mother. She has fever.'

Padma, who had last seen her Amma frying pakoras in the kitchen, tried to look like an anxious daughter.

Gul Chachi was sitting by her bedroom window and turned a sad and anxious face towards them. Tarana hurried to her saying, 'Adaab Chachi, how are you?' She put the tooth powder on the bedside table. 'Dadi sent the powder you had ordered. And I have come to check about your backache…'

The old woman seemed to cheer up as Tarana fussed around her, making her open her mouth to check her teeth, taking her pulse and then bending to check Chachi's back. All the while Tabassum stood nearby, watching and listening like a policewoman. Chachi answered Tarana's questions but otherwise she was very quiet. With Tabassum's back to her, Padma quietly slipped out of the room.

She walked down a corridor, her heart beginning to thud as she expected Tabassum to follow her at any time. She found the kitchen at the back of the house. She ran to the shelf next to the gas stove and after a small attack of panic she found the jar of salt. Taking the paper packet out of her jeans pocket, she poured the powder into the jar and then shook it vigorously to mix it. Dropping the empty packet into the garbage bin she came out thinking, 'Now what do I steal? Tarana said it has to be something they touch often.'

She peered into a bedroom and there on a bedside table there was a string of prayer beads. She grabbed them, quickly stuffing them into her jeans pocket and then walking quickly to the door of Chachi's room as Tabassum turned to look at her.

'I'll wait outside, Tarana didi,' Padma said and walked away.

Outside, as she took a deep breath in relief, she noticed that the boys were nowhere around but the red string was wrapped around a small jacaranda tree. Then on her way out to the lane, she went past the clothes drying on the line and took a quick sniff and smelled roses and jasmines... The boys were peering at her from the gate and she nodded, pulling out the prayer beads with a grin.

Tarana came hurrying out and Padma gave her the beads, as the boys reported that all the jobs were done.

'Good! Let's tell Dadi.'

As they walked back, the children were talking excitedly but Tarana was silent until Dhani asked, 'Is everything okay?'

'No, it's not!' Tarana sighed. 'I'm so angry I could spit and curse and that is not a good idea at all! Just let me walk and calm down.'

'Okay.'

Tarana stood before Banno Bi, who was sitting in the veranda smoking a hookah. 'Dadi, I saw bruises on Gul Chachi's arms and on her cheek as if she had been slapped. She whispered to me that she hurt her back when she was dragged inside that day. And I think she is not eating properly because she is worried her food may be poisoned. Tabassum was standing close by so I could not ask more but I am sure Tabassum is hurting her.'

Banno Bi let off a stream of smoke from her nose, 'Let's see if your ittar works, otherwise I'll have to call my djinns.'

'I felt so angry I nearly cursed that stupid woman but I did not!'

'Why not? Curses that help people are good.'

'You know I don't like them.'

'Of course Tarana, my stupid naturopath! But the world is full of evil and sometimes you have to fight them with djinns and curses.'

'My djinns will work, you wait and see. And my flower spells too.'

Dhani smiled. 'Djinns, curses, spells, you two really are witches, aren't you?'

The two women laughed and refused to reply.

As they walked home, Shahid said glumly, 'Wait and see, nothing will happen.' And for the next week nothing did. They were standing outside Padma's house discussing if it was time to talk to their parents about the Gul Chachi problem when they saw Tarana hurrying down the lane.

'Come along! Barkat Ali and Tabassum are coming to meet Dadi in a few minutes. They called me in the morning.' And they went skipping along, their hearts full of hope.

Banno Bi, senior witch and djinn woman, was ready for a consultation. She was sitting in the living room on a throne-like chair and smoking her hookah. Today she really looked dangerous, the kajal painted darker around her eyes, and she wore four large rings and an armful of bangles that jangled as she smoked. Her dupatta was jet black. Her white cat sat at her feet and gave everyone a beady eye.

Soon Barkat Ali and Tabassum arrived. Tabassum looked unhappy to see the children and muttered, 'Can't we talk to you alone, Begum?'

'No, you can't!' Banno Bi's voice had a strange echo. 'These are all my children and they will bear witness before Allah! He always listens to me.'

Shahid bent his head and swallowed a laugh. 'Poor Allah,' he thought, 'being ordered about by Banno Bi.'

'So what is the problem?' Banno Bi asked through swirling hookah smoke. 'Who's ill? What's the complaint?'

Barkat Ali, a thin, weak-looking man in a fancy

shirt and trousers, said with a small quaver in his voice, 'We are in trouble, Begum. Someone has put a spell on us and only you can help us.'

Banno Bi frowned, 'Why would anyone do that? Have you made anyone angry?'

As Barkat looked confused, Tabassum spoke, sounding surprisingly polite, 'We can't sleep at night and I keep getting nightmares.'

'Someone tied a red thread around a tree.'

'The food tastes strange as if it is all bitter. I have no appetite.'

'My stomach rumbles all the time.'

'Yesterday I put on a kurta and it had ittar on it. I do not use ittar.'

'Now I can't find my prayer beads. How can I pray without my beads?'

By then they were sitting at Banno Bi's feet, clutching her legs as the cat watched in surprise. Barkat Ali was close to weeping.

'Nightmares?' Banno Bi asked. 'They come to warn us not to sin. What have you been doing for the djinn of nightmares to enter your home?' Then she thundered suddenly, making everyone jump. 'Are you hurting someone?' She closed her eyes and whispered, 'I can hear someone crying...'

'It's my fault,' Tabassum mumbled, 'I have not taken care of my mother-in-law... I am so sorry...'

'You have been hitting her?' Banno Bi asked and Tabassum nodded. 'Not giving her good food?' She nodded again, her head hanging low.

Barkat Ali sprang up, staring at his wife in shock, 'What! You hit Ammi? How dare you hit my mother?' He looked so furious Tabassum began to back away nervously.

'But you said we have to make her sell the house… and my father said I have to scare her… what could I do when you earn nothing and she won't give me any money? Always complaining about my cooking…'

'SHUT UP!' Barkat Ali was suddenly all swollen up in rage. 'You go back to your father's home. I don't want to live with you. No one hurts my mother!'

'Wait!' Banno Bi said calmly. 'Her leaving won't make the djinns go away. Gulbadan has to forgive her and she has to serve her mother-in-law and win her trust.' Then she told them what they had to do. First Barkat Ali had to get a job and support his mother and wife. Also, Tabassum had to take care of the house and not fight with anyone. Only when the djinn saw that everyone was happy would it leave the house.

'And change all the masalas in your kitchen,' Tarana said. 'The djinn has obviously poisoned them.'

As the two were leaving, Banno Bi had the last word, 'And remember, if I ever hear the tiniest rumour that my friend Gulbadan is unhappy I'll send my djinns and they are much worse than what you have now.'

'What was in that powder I put in the salt?' Padma wanted to know.

'Banno Bi's masala mix.'

'That gives people nightmares,' Banno Bi was stroking the cat that was now curled in her lap.

'Dried karela powder will make the food taste bitter, make the stomach rumble and give anyone nightmares,' Shahid guessed.

'So would a guilty conscience. The mind can play its own tricks.'

'And the djinn producing ittar?' Dhani asked.

'It's the Flower Power Magic Ittar that can make your dreams come true with the djinn of your choice.' Tarana sat back in a chair, crossed her legs and lit a biri. 'Check my website and order a small bottle for Rs. 350 only. Put a spell on your enemy with the angry djinn. Make anyone fall in love with you through the love djinn. Become rich with the money-making djinn.'

Banno Bi and Tarana laughed, their eyes burning blue in delight.

Dusk was falling in their gali as the three happy, puzzled and amused children wandered home. Shahid had the last word.

'Imagine! It all began because we were flying a kite.'

CHECKMATE

They lied to us and I wasn't surprised. They often do. If the letter had come from Thakurda, my grandfather, we would have been very suspicious but it had been signed by Thamma, my grandma. And here she was coming briskly out of the house to greet us, eyes bright, a big smile, in perfect health and looking both delighted and surprised.

'I knew it... I knew it...' Ma muttered in a fierce whisper.

'Then why didn't you say so?' Baba wanted to know, and I thought it was a perfectly fair question.

It was December 1922 when Shankarda, the manager of the Bose zamindari, had come to our house in Calcutta with a letter from Thamma. She had dictated the letter, of course, as she can barely read or write. It said that she was seriously ill and wanted to see us all. The letter was signed in her awkward scrawl, 'Mrinalini Debi'. So we had packed our bags and taken the early morning train to Tribeni, our family home and she appeared at the door of the mansion as we were getting out of the tonga.

Thamma was plump and soft, with large gentle eyes and lips that now curved in a smile. She always wore white cotton sarees with colourful borders and a sindoor bindi glowed on her forehead along with the sindoor in the parting of her hair. When I was younger, I loved to crawl into her bed and she would hug me close as I fell asleep.

'Oh what a wonderful surprise!' Thamma was exclaiming as smacking kisses landed on my brother's cheeks and mine, 'Sharat... Saraswati...'

Baba frowned, 'Ma, you did not know we were coming?'

Thamma looked a bit confused and then she covered up quickly, 'Your father must have told me, Dhiren. You know how it is... I forget...'

We all looked at each other and knew that this was the work of my revered grandfather. When he wants something he stops at nothing, not even making Thamma sign a letter she had not read—and she would obey unquestioningly because he does not like to be defied. As Ma says, Thamma is a 'traditional Hindu wife'.

That is why we live in Calcutta.

We are the Bose family, zamindars of the village of Tribeni. The head of the family is my grandfather

Shashank Shekhar Bose. His wife is the Mrinalini Debi who was now chattering away as she led us inside. My father is their only son, Dhirendra Shekhar, and his wife, my Ma, is Kasturi—no debi, I'm afraid—because the family does not approve of her. Then there is me, Saraswati, and my younger brother whose full name is actually Sharat Shekhar but he plans to shorten it to just Sharat. Thakurda does not know about that.

Baba and Thakurda have been at war since before I was born. It started when Baba, showing total indifference to the zamindari business, decided to go to Calcutta to study at the Presidency College and then began to teach there. Thakurda had allowed him the college education but now wanted him to come back and help him manage the estate. Then Baba joined the Indian National Congress Party and in 1905 joined the protests against the partition of Bengal. Thakurda, a loyal servant of the British Raj, did not approve. Baba also told Thakurda that he had no intention of becoming a zamindar and exploiting poor farmers. As Thamma told us later, days of yelling followed and Baba went back to Calcutta.

The headline battle began when Baba decided to marry a colleague, a history lecturer called Kasturi. She was not only the wrong caste, belonged to a middle-class family and had a dusky complexion, but was also a child widow. Thakurda was in such a rage that they say he broke half a dining set of china bowls and plates as Thamma just sat in her puja room and cried and cried.

Ma was allowed to step across the threshold of the Tribeni mansion only because Baba refused to enter until she was invited in. All this happened fifteen years ago and Thakurda is still mad at Ma because he is convinced that she is the one who forced Baba to marry her. As always, it was the woman's fault.

In the middle of this endless war is my gentle Thamma who loves us and is kind to Ma. She says that trying to keep the peace in the Bose household is turning her hair white. Sharat and I love her absolutely, Ma adores her and that does not make Thakurda happy. He also knows that if Thamma wrote to Baba asking him to come to Tribeni he would obey.

We all trooped in, past the drawing room or baithak full of heavy dark furniture, gloomy paintings on the wall and dusty shelves with ancient books. Then we came to the open courtyard where all the servants were waiting to greet us with big smiles.

As we walked along the long corridor with a floor of black and white marble squares, I heard Ma ask Baba a question, 'Why has he got us here so urgently, do you think? Your father never does anything without a reason.'

Baba nodded. 'I'm wondering too. He's planning something…'

Thakurda had planned well. It was the Christmas holidays and our schools and Ma and Baba's college were closed. So we had no excuse to head back to Calcutta quickly. Sharat and I loved the house. It had a mango orchard, a pond full of fish, a garden, cows mooing away in the cow shed and Thakurda's old horse called Bantu in the stables. Shankarda said Bantu was 'retired' and seemed to spend his time happily chewing the grass in the orchard. Whenever he saw Thakurda he would clatter up expecting to be fed carrots.

It would have been a happy home if Thakurda did not battle with Baba over everything. Thamma often said that the world would be a better place if we did not have stubborn men with no common sense.

The cook had quickly made breakfast and after a meal of luchi and potatoes with cumin, we went to the living room called chhoto baithak to greet Thakurda. This was the old-style baithak with a huge mattress with a white sheet covering the floor. On it there were white bolsters and Thakurda ruled his world from here, sitting there in his white dhoti and kurta, his moustache bristling across a wide, fleshy face. Beside him were the cash box and the teetering piles of red covered hishaab khatas where Shankarda noted down all the details of the income and expenses of the estate. Baba called the chhoto baithak the centre of feudal patriarchy. I looked it up in the dictionary; it meant a landowning class that is ruled by men. That was my Thakurda all right.

Shashank Shekhar sat exactly as he always did—leaning against a bolster, smoking his hookah, the aroma of the amburi tobacco filling the room. He was listening to Shankarda reading the day's newspaper aloud and occasionally making a sarcastic comment. As we entered, he tried to look grim but his face cracked in a smile when he saw Sharat who was his favourite. Sharat scrambled up on the mattress to go and sit on his lap and get hugged and kissed. I just reached down and touched his feet and felt a perfunctory touch on my head as he very politely blessed me.

Ma covered her head with her sari pallav and bent her head to touch Thakurda's feet. His blessing was quick and silent as he rarely spoke to her. Baba followed and got the same treatment as Thakurda made it clear once again that he was only pleased to see Sharat. Then Baba, Ma and I left the room without starting a conversation as behind me I heard Sharat begin to chatter with Thakurda.

Baba wasn't going to give up, of course. At lunch, sitting before the shiny brass plates and bowls, with Thamma bustling about supervising the maids who were serving us, he stared calmly at Thakurda and said, 'Ma had no idea we were coming. So I think you made her sign that letter without reading it out to her.'

'Ooof Dhiru…' Thamma tried to stop him.

'I wanted to see my family,' Thakurda said, busy eating and not even bothering to raise his head. 'You would have never come if I had written to you.'

'Not to see your family, just your grandson. The others don't matter.'

'Ooof please, Dhiru!' Thamma tried again.

'Well, I know Sharat will take over the zamindari from me one day. So he needs to see his estate.'

'Sharat will go to college and get a job.'

Ma was silent all through. She never spoke up when Thakurda was around. She loved cooking and often cooked at Tribeni but no one ever told Thakurda which dishes had been prepared by her because then it was possible he would rudely push the bowls away. When I was younger, I used to be a bit scared of him but I'm beginning to think he is rather a stupid man, the way bullies usually are.

Thamma asked, 'Why did you call them so urgently, saying I am ill?'

Thakurda refused to answer, yelling at the maid to get him more rice instead; the closed look on his face made me sure he was up to no good.

I had learnt early that girls were not important to my revered grandpa. He was kind when he noticed me, in an absent-minded polite manner, but I seemed to bore him. He would take Sharat with him when he went out to the rice fields to meet the farmers, with Sharat often riding Bantu. They would sit for hours fishing by the pond or watching birds in the orchard but he never invited me.

I wondered why it was so. Was it because I had dusky skin like Ma while Sharat had the pale complexion of the Bose family? The Bose men always married pretty, fair girls, so a dark-skinned widow as a daughter-in-law was a family disaster. Thakurda had learnt nothing from Thamma, who may have been illiterate, but had refused to obey him in loving her daughter-in-law and being proud of her.

Ma once said to me, 'You know I don't mind being called "kalo" because even Ma Kali has dark skin. I hate it when they call my complexion "moyla"—I am not that.'

In Bangla 'kalo' means dark, even black; 'moyla' just means dirty. Even for Thamma, who does love us, we have a moyla skin.

I am a quiet sort of person, the kind that can fade away in a room and so people somehow forget about me. I don't remember either Thakurda or Thamma make a fuss over me like they do with Baba and Sharat. So, next morning people just got busy and left me alone. Baba had gone off to meet his childhood friends in the village. Sharat had accompanied Thakurda on his morning walk to the farms. Thamma and Ma were in the kitchen supervising the cooking and I knew Ma would cook some of the dishes and Thakurda would eat them without comment.

I wandered into the baithak where the sun poured in through the windows and fell on the tall bookcases filled with books that no one read. I opened one of the cases and stared at rows of leatherbound volumes with gold lettering on the spines. Some were in English but most were in Bangla and some in Sanskrit. Baba had told me that his grandfather had been a Sanskrit scholar who taught in a college in Chandernagore, and most of the books belonged to him. Baba had always wanted to be a teacher like his grandfather and I can imagine that did not please Thakurda who said books were a waste of time.

Then I spotted a book of fairy tales, and as I pulled it out, a puff of dust rose up and made me sneeze. I opened the book and on the title page there were two lines in Bangla written in a neat hand, 'This book belongs to Durga Rani Debi. Baro Kalibari, Tribeni'. And then the date with the Bengali calendar year, 'Poila Baisakh, 1280'. I frowned—Durga Rani, who was that?

Carrying the book, I wandered towards the kitchen which was in a block behind the house with a storeroom that held bags of rice, daal and smelled of pungent spices. The vegetables arrived fresh from the farm every morning and Thamma and Ma were sitting in the sunny veranda before the kitchen chopping, slicing and peeling the cabbages, spinach, radishes and potatoes.

'Thamma, who was Durga Rani Debi?' I waved the book. 'I found this in the baithak cupboard, it belonged to her.'

Thamma went on chopping cabbage on the broad iron chopper called bonti. 'Your father's aunt, his pishi.'

'Oh! You mean Thakurda had a sister? How is it we've never met her?'

'She died.'

Ma's hands stopped shelling the peas. 'When did she die? Even your son knows very little about her.'

'Even I know very little,' Thamma said. 'She died before I was married. She had wanted to go to school and studied till class seven and then she was married. She was the youngest, after your Thakurda and the second brother.'

'Thakurda's brother who lives in Jaipur?'

'Yes.' Thamma nodded. 'Durga Rani died young and when I came to this house no one would talk about her. So even I don't know what happened to her.'

I opened the book and stared at her fading handwriting. 'At least she studied until class seven...'

'They used to say she was very bright, did well in school and loved books.' Thamma smiled up at me. 'Just like you.'

I carried the book to my favourite spot in the house, the large squashy sofa in the baithak with its high back behind which I could vanish. A stream of sunlight poured in through the window, with dust motes dancing in the mellow golden rays. I knew that no one would come there and I could read and dream in peace till lunch time.

I slid down into the cushions, opened the book and said, 'Hello Durga Rani, did you like this book?'

And a soft whisper somewhere behind my left ear said, 'Hello Saraswati. Yes, in school that was my favourite book.'

I sat up and whipped around but there was no one there. 'Ww… who was that?'

'Durga Rani. You called me, remember?'

My throat had gone dry, my heart was hammering away against my ribs as I sprang up and whirled around trying to spot her. 'Don't joke please… and I'm not scared…'

There was a short laugh. 'I don't joke and I'm not trying to scare you.' I could hear every word clearly even though the room was empty.

'There are no ghosts!' I declared bravely, wandering around the room peering in the shadows, trying to find someone hiding behind the chairs and cupboards. 'You're hiding somewhere.'

Again I heard that short, impatient laugh. 'Ha! Says a silly little girl from Calcutta.'

'I'm not little. I'm fourteen and NOT silly!' I absently wondered why was I arguing with a bodyless voice.

'This house is full of ghosts. We all meet at the mango orchard on moonless nights. No one who has lived in this house wants to leave.'

I had come to the spot where the voice was strongest, and saw a soft, smoky image that floated and faded before the glass of a bookcase. I could make out the outline of a tall, slim girl in a bright blue sari. Gradually the image grew sharper and I saw an oval face, large eyes and long hair flowing down her back. It was a shimmering, out-of-focus image of a young woman who was smiling at me.

'I can see you a little…'

'If you can then you are not stupid. The idiots of this house can never see me.'

I was no longer feeling scared and settled back on the sofa. Durga Rani followed and sat down at the other end.

'Who are the idiots of this house?'

'Your grandfather, for one. Shashank Shekhar the great zamindar!'

'Thakurda is *stupid*?' I grinned at her. 'He thinks he is a genius who knows the answers to all the questions of the world.'

'Genius? Ha! He never had any brains. I could beat him at chess and cards and as he never read any books, I knew more than him.'

I nodded. Finally I had a friend who understood. 'He is so stupidly stubborn. Imagine, after fifteen years he still won't be nice to Ma. How does that help, you tell me? It just means that Baba stays away from Tribeni.'

'A swollen head does not mean you have more brains...' she said impatiently and we both laughed.

'I think Thamma will agree with you.'

'Your Thamma knows what is right but she will never have the courage to tell him what she thinks of him.'

I smiled at the hazy face before me that wore an irritated frown. 'Clearly you don't like your elder brother.'

Durga Rani laughed.

Just then Sharat poked his head through the door and said, 'Oh there you are! Thamma is calling us for lunch.'

When I turned back Durga Rani had disappeared.

That night at dinner we were all around the dining table with Thamma and Ma hovering around us and serving the dishes. In Tribeni the women always ate later, after playing waitress to the men and children at lunch and dinner. I saw Thakurda take a second helping of the fish in mustard sauce, knowing very well that Ma had cooked it. But would he open his mouth and say that he liked it? Of course not!

Durga Rani was right, he really was a stupid man. Baba was praising Ma and Thamma's cooking and Sharat and I joined in. I watched the old moustachioed gent sitting at the head of the table as he munched away in silence like a cow chewing cud. I realized I was beginning to think a bit like my ghostly great aunt.

Then Thakurda cleared his throat, as if he was going to make an announcement, and to my surprise he turned to me and asked, 'Saraswati, how old are you?'

'Fourteen. I'm going to give my matric examination next year.'

'Good! Then we should think of your marriage now.'

I sat frozen in shock as everyone fell silent.

Finally Baba spoke up, 'Saru is going to college. She is not going to marry now; she is very good in her studies.'

'College?' Thakurda had a strange look of contempt on his face as he said sarcastically, 'A girl going to college? Like her mother?' As if Ma had gone to jail or something.

Then Ma, who was standing behind Baba's chair, spoke very quietly, 'Yes. Like me'

Thakurda stared back at her. 'Your family may have allowed you to go to college, but in my family girls do not study. We know very well that education leads to girls becoming widows, just like you.'

Ma stood still, staring back as her voice remained very calm, 'I studied in college after I was widowed. I was married at the age of eleven and had only been to school.'

Thakurda waved a dismissing hand, 'It is the same. Look at your mother-in-law, she can barely read or write, does that affect her life, eh?' He pushed his chair back and stood up. 'There will be no discussion on this. I have spoken to the Roy Chaudhuri family of Bandel. They are a good Brahmin family and their second son is right for Saraswati. They will be coming to see her tomorrow evening, so make the preparations.'

By then Baba was standing next to Ma, his face red with anger. 'She is my daughter!' he shouted, 'You do not decide anything!'

The two men glared at each other, as Thamma stood frozen at the other end of the table. I noticed that she was twisting her sari between her fingers and her eyes were full of tears. So far she had not uttered a single word.

'If you stop me, Dhiru,' Thakurda went on, 'I'll change my will and leave the estate to my brother, your uncle Satyendra. And I will make sure that you are not allowed to enter this house ever again.'

We all stared at him in shock. Ma was looking anxiously at Baba as my heart began to thud. We all knew how much he loved the Tribeni house and the people in the village. Then I thought in growing panic, he couldn't possibly give up so much for me?

'And,' Thakurda continued blandly, looking very satisfied at the effect he had on all of us, 'I'll never allow you to meet your mother.'

Thamma moved forward now and came to stand before Thakurda, staring at his face. 'You are mistaken. I do not like being an illiterate and if you had allowed me I would have liked to go to school. Saraswati will go to college like her mother did.'

'You stay out of this, Mrinal…' Thakurda began to shout.

'No I won't!' Thamma's voice was shaking a bit but she stood firm. 'You did not even ask me before talking to the Roy Chaudhuris. Tomorrow you will send Shankar to Bandel and cancel the invitation.' She paused to take a breath, 'Or I am leaving with Dhiru and not coming back. Who are you to stop me from meeting my son?'

Thakurda pushed back his chair, stood up and marched out of the room as Ma turned and hugged Thamma and both of them began to cry. Well, one mystery was solved, I thought, now we knew why he had made us come to Tribeni.

That night I lay in bed, not able to fall asleep. I desperately wanted to go back to Calcutta because I was so afraid of Thakurda. I was sure he would come up with something else to hurt Ma and the thought of it made me very afraid.

Next morning, I desperately needed to talk to Durga Rani, my great-aunt, so I went to the baithak, opened the book of fairy tales and whispered, 'Durga Rani, where are you?'

'Right here!' a perky little whisper in my ear and there she was, a shimmering girl sitting on the sofa beside me.

'You heard what happened yesterday?' She shook her head and I told her about the scary dinner. 'Imagine what would have happened if Baba and Ma had obeyed Thakurda? I could never go to college.'

She frowned, 'In our family they name the girls after goddesses and then they treat them like slaves. You are named after Saraswati, the goddess of learning, and that fool wants to stop you from going to college. I am not surprised.'

'I wonder how many illiterate Saraswatis there are in our country...' I brooded.

'I would always come first in my class but I was only allowed to go to the village school while Shashank Shekhar was sent to the Christian school in Chandernagore. The horse carriage would take him to school every day and...' she began to laugh, 'he failed twice in his matric exams and then got a third division. My father was furious.'

We shared a grin. 'Now I understand why he does not like Ma. She got the Governor's Gold Medal after her post graduate in History.'

'Also she can cook and run a house, work that is expected of all good Indian wives...'

'And knit and stitch and sing.'

'She scares our Shashank Shekhar. And so do you.' Durga Rani was beginning to fade before me. 'So stop being afraid of what he thinks of you. Fight him!'

'Durga Rani, how old were you when you died?' I had to ask her the questions that had been swirling in my head from the moment I had met her, 'What happened to you?'

The pale face stilled. 'I was your age, fourteen. My father was not too keen but mother and Shashank Shekhar insisted that I was getting too old and had to be married off. My dear brother really wanted me to be out of the house.' I had noticed before that she never called her brother 'dada', always that ironic Shashank Shekhar.

'No one listened to my begging to let me study. In my husband's home they made me do all the housework—wash, clean and cook; collect water and feed the cows. The smoke in the kitchen gave me a cough and no one called a doctor and then I died.'

'Oh Durga Pishi…' I whispered, my throat going all tight with tears.

'They did not have a single book in that house, so I came back here. And I stay here in the baithak where I can read the books. No one comes here anyway. It's just that I'm running out of books… The Sanskrit ones are very hard to understand.' She gave a small laugh, 'That's the problem with being a very old ghost.'

'Don't go away,' I said urgently and ran to my room, then came back with all the books and magazines that Ma, Baba and I had brought to Tribeni over the years. 'Next time I'll get a bag full of books for you.'

'Oooh! So many new writers… Sarat Chandra, Bankim Chandra… who is Rabindranath Tagore? A poet? Oh thank you so much!'

By then she was a shadow against the book cases and as I watched, my great-aunt and friend vanished.

In the evening, I wandered into the chhoto baithak and a familiar scene. Shankarda was playing chess with Thakurda and as always the old man was yelling at him. I think Shankarda is quite a good player but Thakurda bullies him so much he gets nervous and makes mistakes. Or maybe he thinks it is safer to lose than listen to the old man's sarcastic comments. He worked for Thakurda after all and could not risk angering the old man.

I perched beside Shankarda and as he reached for the horse I said, 'No. Move the bishop and block the queen.'

Thakurda glared at me, 'Since when have you become a chess player?'

'Since I was eight and Baba taught me… cut that pawn….'

With a happy sigh Shankarda snapped up Thakurda's pawn and grinned at me, 'Arrey you are clever, Saru!'

I was looking straight at Thakurda, 'I am and I'll pass my matric in the first division. Just you wait and see.'

He was staring back with a mean, slit-eyed look, 'Oh you will? Will you now!'

'I am going to study and teach, just like Ma. No one will stop me. I'm not going to die coughing in a smoky kitchen.'

That's when he flinched and lowered his eyes.

I wasn't going to stop even as I sensed Shankarda sitting still beside me, listening to us. 'I have never failed in school. Never. And neither has Ma.'

He looked up and glared at me again, his cheeks beginning to turn red. 'I thought you were a silent little mouse. You have suddenly found your voice, haven't you?'

I pointed to the chess board. 'Move the queen, Shankarda.' He moved it fast to the square before the king. 'Checkmate, Thakurda!'

Shankarda laughed.

SNiFF AND TELL

In the car, as we headed out of Delhi airport, my revered mother turned to me, knitted her plucked eyebrows, and said, 'I'd be *extremely* grateful, Arjun, if you would occasionally smile and…'

'… remember to say "please and thank you". Yeah, I heard you. I will.' She had said that to me at least six times on the plane.

The guard at the gate of the house spotted her in the car, saluted and ran to open the huge metal gates and Mum looked thrilled. She loves it when people salute her. As we reached the main door it was opened by the housekeeper, a grim-faced woman who never smiles, so I did not have to exercise my facial muscles either. We were led up to the guest bedrooms with the driver carrying in our bags. The housekeeper told us dinner would be served at eight-thirty and left us alone.

I wandered around my room. It smelt breezy—of room freshener and of the vase of roses on the writing table. Cool. I collapsed on the bed, lying flat on my back staring up at the ceiling and sighing in despair. The smells were going to come soon enough. A whole endless fortnight of this… I could hardly bear the thought and I had suffered this every year since I could remember.

Dad and I have tried to make Mum understand that they don't really want us to visit them but she refuses to believe us. 'They' are my uncle Chandrakant or Chandu Mama, his wife Uma Mami and their two wonderful kids—the slow and sleepy Sagar and the weird and hyper Ruchika. Chandu Mama is Mum's older brother and she thinks the sun rises from his posterior because he is a super rich businessman and lives in a mansion in Delhi's super posh Shanti Niketan. My Dad is just a lecturer in physics and we live in the staff quarters of a college in Lucknow.

Every summer holiday she drags me to Delhi to spend time with them even though technically speaking, they have never invited us. And I mean *never*. It is supposed to be all about bonding, she with her brother and sister-in-law and me with my beloved cousins. But they are both older than me and behave as if I don't exist.

Sagar occasionally goes to work at Chandu Mama's factory. Mostly he just loiters around the house with headphones inserted in his ears, spends ages combing his hair and has an awesome collection of colognes.

His Facebook page is full of pouting girls and men leaning against motorbikes. Ruchika is supposed to be studying in college but usually gets up at noon and drives off with her friends. I have never seen either of them read a book. They both only take partying seriously. I have nothing to say to them and they can't be bothered to talk to me. Some bonding.

Next year, I get to class eleven and to my relief Dad has laid down the law that I have to study for my board exams. So this was hopefully going to be my last trip to this mansion-cum-five-star hotel where I choke at the smells that drift around in the air. The odours in the two drawing rooms, television room, my uncle's den, my aunt's coffee room, the dining room, two kitchens and eight bedrooms...

Smell. Odour. Aroma... I am always conscious of them, on people and in houses. My super sensitive nose can not only detect a smell, it can also sniff out its character. Is it a good smell or an evil one, an ordinary odour or something weird? And in this house the smells are everywhere—a thin layer of fumes that float like an invisible fog a few feet above my head, and I get a whiff of it as I walk about. Sometimes it is oily and cloying like a musk perfume and gives me a headache, at others it has the reek of rotting garbage and is so strong it makes me gag. Most of the time it is just a faint touch of bitterness in the air, like an unnamed gas.

Only I can smell it and I don't know why this house smells the way it does, when the maids are always dusting and mopping and there are flowers in every room.

Since I was a kid, I've known that houses have odours and they smell bad when the people who live in them are in some sort of trouble—unhappy, fighting or angry. For example, I hate going into the home of my friend Raghu, though we have been playing together in the park virtually all our lives. His home smells of his mother's illness. There is something wrong with her mind. Mum says she suffers from depression but Dad thinks it is something much more serious. She drags around the house, her hair uncombed, eyes all glassy and looking like a ghost. His home smells of ashes and mouldy biscuits and it makes me so sad.

As we came down to dinner I got ready to smile as finally Chandu Mama and Uma Mami would make an appearance. I knew my cousins wouldn't be around, because standing at my window I had seen them drive off in their cars, all sleek in party gear. A few times, because my Mum made an issue of it, Sagar has taken me along to pubs where he and his gang drink until they can barely stand, laugh loudly at utterly idiotic jokes and try to hit on the girls on the dance floor. Nowadays I say a polite no and he is visibly relieved about that. Ruchika has never taken me anywhere and she usually acts as if I don't exist, which is just fine by me.

Mum sprang up from the sofa with a huge smile and went to air kiss Uma Mami who hates being touched. Mami has a really interesting face. Everything on it droops, the corner of her mouth, the eyes, the cheeks. She always wears flappy pants and loose flowery shirts and her fingers are loaded with huge rings. Her hair is dyed an unnatural shade of black and she always carries a purse around with her that jangles with keys.

I got up very, very slowly and gave my best, bared teeth smile, 'How are you Uma Mami? You look well.'

She turned her large, yellowy eyes towards me, did not return my smile and said, 'Oh do I?' So far she hadn't said a word to Mum and now turned to ask, 'Drink, Bibi? Gin and lime?'

Mum gave a ghastly giggle. 'Oh Uma! I'd love a gin.' Actually, Mum doesn't really like alcohol but don't expect her to admit that to Mami.

'And you Arjun?' the eyes flicked towards me.

'A Pepsi, please.'

She waved vaguely at a young maid standing by the door who went off to get my drink. The cola would arrive in a heavy cut glass tumbler that I am often tempted to drop on the floor to see if it breaks or not. Mami has that effect on me.

As Mami poured, I noticed the gin in her glass was about twice the amount of that in Mum's. Then Chandu Mama came bustling in, plump, fair and balding, rubbing his hands as if anticipating something exciting.

'Ah Arjun! The family genius! How are your studies going?'

'Good! I plan to try for the IITs after the boards.'

'Good! Good!'

We have this conversation *every* summer.

He settled beside Mum and soon they were chattering away. Uma Mami helped herself to more gin as I sipped the Pepsi and finished a bowl of peanuts. Then I got a whiff of something like bad breath floating in the air.

Sometimes, very rarely, I also get a weird flash with a smell, like a jerky movie flashing before my eyes. Last year one of the boys from the tenth grade named Anshu was found injured and unconscious in the gym, but when he woke up in hospital he couldn't remember anything. I was feeling very upset because he was a good chap. The next day I wandered into the gym and immediately smelled the stink, like a blocked sewer. As I was staring at the spot where Anshu was found, there was a flash and I could clearly see a twelfth grade bully called Kapil come up behind him and hit him with a cricket bat.

I sat there, scared and shaking, not knowing what to do. Who would believe me? I had no proof. And if Kapil found out I had snitched on him I was dead. Luckily one boy in Kapil's gang panicked when the police began to question them and spilled the beans.

That flash comes very rarely and I can't bring it on even if I tried. I never know when it will come as it is *totally* out of my control.

By the time we sat down to dinner Uma Mami had a slight sway to her walk. The khansama, all stiff and starchy in a white uniform served the meal. This was the only part of the visit I liked. They had a fabulous cook and the food was absolutely out of this world.

Mum took a mouthful of the mushroom pulao and exclaimed, 'Oh Uma, this is delicious!'

Uma Mami raised those amazing droopy eyes and stopped chewing, so her jowls stopped shaking and snapped, 'Tell the chef. I didn't cook it.'

'Have some more…' Chandu Mama said quickly. Then his mobile rang and for the rest of the meal he muttered away about sales budgets and meetings and then said something about the 'trip to Chennai'.

'Oh Bhaiya!' Mum tried to look all heartbroken. 'Are you travelling?'

'Have to leave for Chennai tomorrow morning, Bibi, and I don't know when I'm back. But you have a good time.' I knew what that meant. He'll give her a wad of cash, fix a car and driver to take her around and Mum will go *totally* berserk shopping. Uma

Mami will make excuses about her 'meeting at the club' or her 'appointment with the dentist' and never go with her.

Once I heard Mami on the phone say, 'Chandrakant's awful sister Bibi is here again and she'll go shopping every day. You wouldn't believe her taste in clothes! It gives me a headache just watching her buy all those cheap, shiny suits from Lajpat Nagar.'

Mum couldn't care less. Luckily for me, nowadays she is perfectly happy going off alone. Earlier she used to drag me along and I would sit in shops for hours fiddling with my Rubik's Cube as she looked at clothes, bed covers, shoes, jewellery, make up... I know Dad hates her taking money from Chandu Mama but she never listens to him. Whenever Dad comes to Delhi, which is very rarely, he stays with his sister, my Lila Bua, because he says he likes to feel welcome.

Next morning after breakfast I saw off Mum, headed out of the house and stepping on to the road took a deep breath of relief. I could finally breathe properly. Then I began a slow, happy stroll towards the narrow lanes of Munirka and one tiny apartment that was guarded by a lazy cat.

Dad's older sister, my Lila Bua opened the door and we smiled, studying each other. 'New haircut.' I pointed to her grey head of close-cropped hair.

'Well I'm sort of going bald.'

'Like hell you are. You're always looking for excuses to cut your hair short.'

She ran her fingers through her salt and pepper crew cut. 'Good hair style; doesn't need much combing.'

Her brown and white cat wandered up to listen to us. 'Oye Button! Kaisa hai, fatty?' He looked insulted and stalked off.

Bua was chopping veggies at her dining table and went back to slicing beans. 'Your Mum's off shopping I suppose.'

'Yup.' I was hunting for the television remote. 'Sarojini Nagar, South Extension, lunch with a friend at Khan Market... Full programme.'

'Met your cousins yet?'

'Nope. Late night partying, they were not up yet.'

'And how's your Uma... expletive deleted... Mami?'

'Seriously into gin and tonic and Chandu Mama asks the same questions and doesn't listen to my replies.' I lay back on her comfy divan, stuffed a cushion under my head, picked up a book and sighed with happiness.

'So you are having fun.'

'I am. That's why I am here. Can we stop that bean cutting and onion peeling and order Thai food?'

'Can do.' And with great relief she dropped the knife and put all the veggies back in the fridge. She hates cooking, is a god-awful cook, and she doesn't even apologize about it. Once Dad commented that her dark brown meat curry tasted of mobile oil and she grinned and said, 'Now how did you discover my cooking secret, dear brother?' So the best strategy is to move quickly and fix a takeout menu.

I lay back, closed my eyed and sniffed. A faint touch of jasmines… And freshly baked bread… happy smells here, always.

Over tom yum soup, green fish curry and phad thai noodles Bua said, 'You can always stay with me. The Great Shopaholic won't even notice you are missing for the next few days.'

'That's the plan. I'll meet Sagar and Ruchika at dinner, then they'll be busy… Chandu Mama left for Chennai today and…'

'Uma… expletive deleted… Mami will have her kitty party.'

'You adore her, dontcha?'

'Oh *absolutely*! Chandrakant married her because she was the only daughter of an industrialist and she never lets him forget it. Poor git.'

'Have you noticed she never smiles?'

'How can she? It may give people the wrong idea.'

'Huh? What wrong idea?'

'… that she likes you. Then you'll ask her for a loan or steal her money. She thinks the whole world is after her money.'

We were now concentrating on the phad thai, which

I believe is the best noodle dish in the world. 'Did you know he has a girlfriend?'

'Who? Sagar?'

'Nope.' God! It's such fun gossiping with Bua. 'Chandu Mama.'

Her fork froze halfway to her mouth, strands of noodles hanging in mid-air as she grinned, 'Oh *does* he? *Good* for him!'

'Saw her at a party last year, sort of fair and plump…'

'How did you know she was the girlfriend?'

'Ruchika pointed her out to me and said, "That's my dad's latest… ummm… girlfriend".'

Bua, popped a prawn into her mouth. 'That Ruchika is a very strange girl.'

'Snooty and really bad-tempered, yeah, but strange? Nah!'

'She is. Remember last winter Uma's cousin's daughter was getting married?'

'Mum got typhoid and couldn't make it and drove Dad batty.'

'To my surprise Uma had sent me a card and your silly Mum called up and insisted that I had to go. So I did, in my one and only thirty-year-old silk sari.'

'God! Was Mum upset when the doctors said she couldn't travel! She had new clothes all ready and plans to dance at the sangeet… she moaned for weeks and weeks.'

'Well it was at the sangeet that I saw Ruchika behave very strangely. First she refused to dance and had to be dragged to the stage...'

'They had a dance *stage*?'

'Yeah and a disc jockey.'

'A DJ Bua, we call 'em DJ.'

'Whatever. Then there were endless film songs, all these kids thinking they were film stars, jiggling their bums and looking truly silly.'

'So what did Ruchika do?'

'Well, first she refused to dance and then once she started she wouldn't stop. The songs ended, everyone began to walk away but she kept on whirling and twirling till Sagar pulled her away and then she created a really nasty scene, screaming at him.'

'Drunk, was she?'

Bua shrugged. 'Who knows? She was on something, that's for sure... It's sad, because she is not stupid like Sagar, who isn't exactly genius material...'

I began to laugh. 'Sagar Bhaiya once asked me if we need a visa to go to Mizoram. He thought it was in Korea.'

'Ha! You made that up.'

'No! Honest to god! And he thought Naxalites came from Pakistan.'

'What a waste. These kids get the best education, such wonderful opportunities and they do nothing worthwhile. That Ruchika has a good brain and she is allowing it to rot… lazy fools.'

'Uma Mami thinks her children are perfect.'

'She would.'

'Ruchika's really rude to her.'

'That girl should be woken up every morning with a dozen tight slaps to make her see some sense.'

'Ha! Some hope.'

I headed back to Chandu Mama's house for dinner, my heart sinking at the thought of a meal in the wonderful company of Mami, Sagar and Ruchika all squabbling away. As I was entering the house, I got a feeling something was not right. I had to push open the heavy gate as the guard was missing. Then I noticed the lights blazing in the drawing room. As I reached the main door, which was also open, I heard Uma Mami screaming.

The drawing room was full of people. My Mum and Sagar were sitting on a sofa, Mum sitting up straight looking a bit anxious and Sagar slumped back with a slight smile, as if watching an amusing show. Ruchika was in a chair, one leg hooked over an arm with her usual bored expression.

Sagar was saying in this irritated drawl, 'Oh shut up, Mummy! You are wrong! Leave the servants alone.'

Uma Mami was pacing up and down in front of all her staff who were standing in a line in front of her like prisoners—the guard, cook, khansama, housekeeper and two maids. They were all staring at her with wide eyes as she screamed the worst abuses I have ever heard. I didn't even know the meaning of some of the Punjabi words she was using. Then I saw Mum's eyes widen in shock at something she said; it must have been really bad.

'Sagar Bhaiya,' I bent over him and whispered. 'What's up?'

'Usual craziness. She thinks someone's stolen her money.'

'It's happened before?'

'Many times, but small amounts. This time she says its thirty grand.'

The khansama said gently, 'Memsahib how can anyone steal? We do not enter your room unless you are there. You ordered us, remember?'

'We don't even know where your money is kept,' the housekeeper added. 'And you always carry your keys.'

Suddenly Mami came to a stop in front of one of the maids, a gentle-faced girl who was looking very scared, and hissed, 'You! I know you stole it. You cleaned my room yesterday. Get out! Pack your bags and go!'

The girl's eyes flooded with tears. 'I did not, ma'am. You were there all the time while I was cleaning…'

The housekeeper tried to intervene, 'She may be new, ma'am, but she is a very good girl and she won't lie. I know her mother…'

'Sagar!' Mami whipped around and yelled. 'Call the police!'

To his credit Sagar did not move, as the girl, shaking with fear, began to cry.

I sniffed. The room was really smelly, like a dead rat giving off putrid fumes. I wandered past the servants and it wasn't them, though I got a whiff of the sweaty reek of fear. I drifted past Sagar and caught the aroma of cigarettes and cologne and then behind Mum who had on her flowery perfume.

Finally I was standing near the chair where Ruchika was sitting. As I got closer, the smell got stronger. She sat there, one leg dangling and the foot jiggling away as if it had a life of its own. She was chewing gum and staring at the maid as if the crying girl was a display in a zoo. The poor girl was now standing before Mami with her hands folded, begging that she should not call the police.

'Sack her, Mummy!' Ruchika gave a high-pitched laugh. 'Sack that stupid cow! Sack everyone!' Clearly, she was finding it all very funny.

The rotting smell was nearly choking me… And then flash!

I turned to her and said really loudly so that

everyone could hear me, 'You took the money, didn't you Ruchika didi?'

Everyone froze and all the faces turned towards me as Ruchika straightened, her eyes turning into shiny, evil slits. 'What do you mean, you moron? Shut up!'

I sniffed. Flash!

'Uma Mami was in the bathroom. You took her keys from her purse and opened the cupboard, the one next to her dressing table, and took out a brown paper packet that was under her clothes...'

As Ruchika sprang up, her eyes widening, Mami turned to me, 'How dare you, Arjun! Apologize now!'

Somewhere in the background I could hear Mum's helpless voice saying softly, 'Arjun, what are you *saying*? Stop *please*...'

Ruchika and I were facing each other like two fighters. She smelled awful! Then Ruchika came closer in a threatening way and I nearly gagged at the stench. Her lips curved downwards in a vicious smile. 'And how do you know about the packet and the cupboard? You took the money, didn't you? Like mother like son... eh?'

I shook my head. 'I was out all day and have just come back.'

Flash!

My heart was thudding and I couldn't breathe, 'You put the packet in a gold purse and drove off in your car.'

Suddenly Sagar was standing next to me, his eyes sharp with interest. 'What did she do next?'

'She drove to a car park and gave some cash to a man in a blue T-shirt and he gave her packets with some pills and white powder in them.' I closed my eyes to remember better, 'Two-thousand rupee notes.'

Ruchika turned to Sagar, 'He is lying, Bhaiya, the creep.'

Flash!

'The rest of the money is in her laptop bag.'

Sagar turned to his sister and I've never seen him look so angry before. 'You are buying drugs again? You promised me you were clean!'

I realized that Uma Mami had stopped screaming, standing frozen before the maid, and everyone in the room was leaning forward, listening with wide eyes. The housekeeper had a slight smile curving her lips, as she nodded at me in approval.

That's when Ruchika launched herself at me, teeth bared like an angry witch, hands reaching out and her nails scoring down my arm. As I stepped back trying to save myself, the khansama and Sagar pulled her away. I didn't feel the bloody scratches much because the smell was choking me and I had to walk away to the other end of the room to breathe.

That night Mum and I packed our bags, called a taxi and shifted to Bua's house. Only the servants came to bid us goodbye and the maid couldn't stop thanking me. The cook gave us a cake and the housekeeper blessed me.

In the car I discovered that the Great Shopaholic was not ready to go home yet as a lot of the cash that she got from Chandu Mamu was still left. I did not protest. Mum is not too good at handling stressful situations and the poor, silly thing was really shook up by all the drama. It was finally dawning on her that these Chandu Mama funded shopping days were over.

Mum said she wasn't hungry and went to bed. Then over a late dinner of leftovers from the fridge and the cake, Lila Bua stared at me. 'How did you know it was Ruchika? Did you follow her to that car park?'

I tried to avoid answering her, busily chewing the cake, acting as if I hadn't heard her.

'Umm, now I know! One of the servants must have told you. They know everything that goes on in a house.'

Okay, let's see how she takes this. 'I can smell evil. Ruchika smelt like a thief. Stank like a decomposing rat.'

Bua laughed, 'Yeah… riiight! Good one, Arjun.'

PAYBACK

They have kept the room exactly as I had left it, except that it is much cleaner now. Then that is Amma, she can never handle a mess. She has to straighten the bed cover, put the books back in the shelves and wipe the table top. Even my toy ET, that she disliked so much, is still sitting on my writing table. Only now he isn't so dusty, his long finger pointing into the void of my useless life.

Amma is always flapping around the house shifting the furniture and I had expected her to soon turn my room into something else—maybe a study for Appa or a guest room—but no, it was still my room and it's now a year since I went away. Twelve months and six days, I calculated quickly. Long enough to be forgotten, I would have thought.

As I have floated and watched this past year, I have often seen Amma enter the room early in the morning before Appa is awake or when he has gone on his morning walk. She stands by my bed or sits on the chair by the writing table looking lost, her eyes holding a dazed sadness that makes me want to reach out and hug her. I even tried once but clearly she did not feel anything. Of course, Amma was never one for hugging. Her life was serious business and she dealt with it by preparing as if going out to battle every day. There were times when Appa and I would be laughing our heads off at a joke and she would give a small puzzled smile, not getting the joke at all, and that made us laugh even harder.

Many evenings when Amma is late from work and Appa is alone at home he comes in and sits at my writing table touching my laptop, opening the desk drawers and staring at the mess of pens, pencils, wires and earphones. They never came into my room so often before, never sat on my bed and cried. Funny I had to end it all to discover that in fact Amma and Appa had really loved me, that they were not ashamed of me at all.

Why didn't they tell me?

That morning I was hovering around them and listening to their conversation as they sat in the garden having their morning cups of coffee. What I heard made me go still in surprise. They were talking about my older brother Kartikeyan coming home from IIT Kanpur for the winter break, something that always got Amma very excited.

'Kartik called last night,' Appa said, 'you were asleep so I didn't wake you.'

'Oh Kartik called!' Amma's hand holding the coffee cup stilled. 'You should have woken me up…'

'You have so much trouble sleeping, I'm grateful when you fall asleep.'

'What did Kartik say?'

'He's coming next week and will stay for six weeks.'

'Six weeks? But the winter break is…'

'He's going to do an internship at Infosys. Remember, he told us he's looking for something in Bangalore?'

Of course, I thought, the great Kartik going to Infosys was no surprise at all.

'I was thinking we'll have to ask around to find him an internship,' Amma's voice had a quiet satisfaction that always creeps in when she speaks of Kartik, her perfect child. 'I should have known he'll do it himself. He always does so.'

'He also wants to meet my friends who are in the IT business. There is two years left in Kanpur but he's already planning his career. I'm sure he won't stay in India.'

Amma nodded. 'He is ambitious, I know.'

Appa said gently, 'You know, in the future you shouldn't expect him to be there for us. Kartik is not Dhani, his love is not as simple…'

Amma stared at him, 'What do you mean by that?'

'Kartik has worked out the direction of his life and as he grows older there will be less space for us in it. Right now he needs us, but later?' Appa shrugged.

'You mean he is selfish.'

Appa shrugged again, 'I would say that. You will say he is focussed.' Then he looked away and I saw his eyes flood with tears. 'Dhani was different, he cared…' Then his voice closed up.

Appa thought I was better than Kartik? How is it I had never known that?

They were silent for a long time and then Amma checked the time on her phone. Ah, work! Nothing gets in the way of that.

I curled up in one of the garden chairs, Appa's words running through my head. Soon they would both leave for work and I'd be alone again. I'm used to that even though I had an older brother. Kartik never had much time for me. When he was in school with me he often stayed back for football and I came back alone to our cook Shakuntala Akka opening the door and serving me lunch. She knew more about what I liked to eat than Amma did. Amma, the paediatrician, only checked the nutrition value of the meals I ate, weighed me and marked my height against a wall in the dining room. If I wanted a snack, or tore my clothes, I went to Shakuntala Akka.

My parents don't talk about me much. The son who has done the bunk, as my friend Kapil would say with his crooked grin. I know that they think of me when they stand in my room, looking stunned and puzzled as if I had hit them over the head with a hammer. But I am not discussed. I think I'm a ghost they are ashamed of and would like to forget. But they can't forget, and that surprises me. They stand there, often next to my neatly-made bed, as if waiting to hear from me.

Why didn't they listen to me when I needed them?

But I have to be honest. How could they listen when I wasn't talking?

It all began when I turned fifteen and Amma said I could join Facebook. I had been begging for months as everyone in my class was talking about friends, posts and tags and I couldn't join in. Of course, it was not as exciting as I had expected it to be. I didn't get as many friends as the others and very few of the girls in class accepted my friend request. I knew why. They did not like me. I had heard a girl describe me as 'Dhananjay, that weirdo'. Even Kapil at times teased and called me 'Dhani the alien'. I knew he was joking but it still hurt.

I would stare at the posts of my classmates at parties, in malls, at movie halls—all looking like they were having a great time. I was never in those selfies.

Once, just trying to join in, I wrote a comment on a post by Ashit of a party in his home, 'You guys seem to be having a great time.'

Ashit replied, 'Wishing you were there, Dhani?'

Did I wish that? I wasn't so sure. Whenever I was invited to a party I would start to worry. What do I wear? Do I arrive on time or half an hour late? What gifts should I take? What do I talk about? Then at the party I would wander around not knowing what to do, or stand at the fringe of a group not finding a way to join in the conversation. I would end up hanging around Kapil and he didn't like having a gloomy shadow either, especially not when he was talking to a girl. I never knew what to do at parties and my heart would sink if anyone invited me. It was really weird, I felt sad if no one invited me and very nervous when anyone did—as always, a problem with no solution.

Once, I remember Kartik was home for the vacations and he was going out all the time, talking about pubs, night clubs and girls. Then I got invited to a party and I accepted just to prove to him that I had friends too. I came back pretty early after mooching around all evening, feeling lost. The moment dinner was served, I ate and then headed for home feeling quite relieved the ordeal was over. Amma and Appa were in bed but Kartik was sprawled on the living room sofa watching a sports channel.

He looked up at me. 'You're back early,' then turning back to the football match he said disdainfully, 'but then you always are.'

Why? Was there a time, a deadline before which I could not leave a party? If I came home early then was I a social disaster he was embarrassed about?

'I got bored and the music was too loud.'

'Learn to dance, bro. Then time goes fast.'

I wonder if Amma and Appa would have understood if I had talked to them about this growing feeling I had that no one liked me because I was a quiet person. I was invisible because I was not good looking. At times even Kapil was embarrassed to be seen with me. I just couldn't find a way to talk to them because the only time we were together was at the dinner table and the conversation went something like this:

Appa: So how was school?

Me: Okay.

Amma: Wasn't it your physics test today? How did it go?

Me: Good I think.

Amma: Take some more fish curry. You're getting too thin, you don't eat enough proteins Dhani, always munching snacks and then you are not hungry at dinner...

Here we go again, nutrition and physics, school and project reports. We three had forgotten how to talk to each other since Kartik left for Kanpur. He was so good at noise and excitement and things to talk about because there was always something happening to him. I was so boring in comparison.

Every morning when I headed to the stop to catch the school bus, I used to see them. A girl who was in Class Seven in our school and her father. She would come walking down the lane with him and they would be talking, arguing and laughing. Looking at them I wished that Appa would sometimes come to the bus stop with me and we could talk about cricket or books or movies like that girl's father did.

Nowadays once Amma and Appa have left for work Shakuntala goes home and comes back in the evening to cook dinner. No one needs lunch anymore. I saw her cry when she said this to Amma, who looked all stony-faced and said nothing. She has never said this to anyone but I think deep inside Amma thinks I was weak, that Kartik would never have given up like I did.

I floated through the closed window of my room from the garden and sat down before my laptop, wondering if as an alien ectoplasm I could make it work. I reached out and tried to open the lid but it stayed closed. My hands, those smoke-like things with shifting fingers, had no grip. I sat and brooded about finding a way to open the laptop. Even ghosts need

Google, and someone had once said that you stayed alive forever on the Internet.

I closed my eyes and began concentrating really hard, thinking fiercely, 'Open up… opppen up…' and to my amazement the lid lifted slowly. I went on concentrating, saying in my mind, 'Switch on… switch onnn…' It came on, the familiar whirling design on the screen shifting and turning before my eyes like an old friend.

'Hello Google, there you are,' I thought in triumph. 'This is mind power, baby.' I was feeling very pleased with myself. Staring at the familiar icons, I was surprisingly happy; but then machines are easy, I could always understand them.

As I touched the keys and the touchpad, I realized that if I stared at them at the same time I could make them move under my fingers. It was a bit slow and not at the speed with which I could use the keys earlier but oh joy! I was using my laptop again. All I had to do was to get my mind to focus on my fingers and it obeyed me. I doodled through my files. There was the half-written essay, the poems I was trying and failing to write, the quiz I had downloaded… it felt so good to be back in my own world. My email inbox had the usual spam, not many people wrote to me anyway.

Then I don't know why I went onto Facebook, entered my password, opened my page and stared at it in surprise.

Why were people still tagging me and writing on my page? Mark Zuckerberg is right, the world is full of idiots. Why were they commenting on my tragic death? 'Our friend Dhananjay.' Really? Since when? Then I saw the endless 'RIP Dhananjay' and I sat there and laughed. Since when does a suicide rest in peace, you bunch of brainless morons?

I stared at the posts from Ashit and Namita. It seems I was their 'dear friend'. I remembered that they had first started calling me the Alien, a name that stuck until the whole class was calling me that. But then what else can you expect from Facebook, where falseness rules, everyone is always dazzlingly happy and your pet alien is transformed into a friend. I was about to leave the page when I saw the latest post. It was from Surendran. We were in the school quiz team.

Surendran had written, 'It is a year since we lost him. If Dhani is not with us anymore it is because we failed him as friends.' I sat still, staring at the words. Quiet, gentle Surendran had liked me enough to remember me a year later. Then he went on, 'Writing sad posts and stupid hashtags now is a waste of time.'

Ashit of course had to respond, 'Failed him? What do you mean by that?'

Surendran: 'Will you say you were a real friend?'

No reply so far from Ashit but right below there

was Kapil. 'Friendship? Ashit Shetty doesn't even know what it means. He thinks bullying is friendship.'

I sat still staring at the next line from Surendran. 'I agree. #AshitShettythebully.'

I checked the date. This conversation had happened two days ago. Why were they writing about me? Why was I still alive in their memories? I should have been long forgotten. Then I remembered. Appa had started a scholarship in my name at school and there had been an announcement at morning assembly.

It looked like I was trending among my classmates.

I got into trouble with Ashit when on an impulse I sent a friend request to Namita, who was officially his girlfriend. Next morning, when I entered the classroom, they were standing at the door surrounded by their gang of suckers. As I went past, Ashit said something I couldn't catch. They stared at me and then they all laughed. My face was hot as I sat down at my desk and Ashit strolled over, looming over me, his hands in his pockets.

'You really think she wants you as a friend, Alien?'

'It's her decision…' I mumbled, keeping my head down.

'Don't even visit her page, okay?'

By then Namita and the others had surrounded me and they all had diabolical grins on their faces. I clenched my hands to stop them from shaking.

Ashit leaned forward, his sneering face inches away from mine. 'Have you looked at yourself in the mirror?'

Namita batted her eyelashes at me and drawled, 'A friend request? Are you in love with me, Monster from Mars?'

Just then Kapil noticed the crowd around me and came up and stared at them. 'What's happening here?'

'We're making friends with an alien,' Namita said offhandedly and then they all drifted away. They always troubled me when I was alone.

Ashit and his gang always picked a target for their bullying games and now it was me. The class watched but except for Kapil no one confronted them. But then why should they? Also, Ashit was clever. He never put anything down in print—no posts, mails, messages or anything on Whatsapp that could be used as a complaint. It was all in school and covered by the excuse of 'teasing'.

When I went past them in the corridors they would make kissing noises or call out, 'Hey Alien!' and I noticed that many of the other kids were grinning. I was quite tall but very thin while Ashit is short and hefty; while going past me in the cafeteria he would deliberately crash into me making me drop my tray of food. Then he would apologize profusely as his gang laughed.

And so it went on, all because of something as innocent as a friend request.

I don't remember when it started, this feeling of emptiness inside, as if I had become invisible and did not really exist. I felt tired all the time and it was a battle getting out of bed every morning. I just wanted to stay in my room but that was not possible, and as the bus got closer to school my throat would close up and I wanted to get out and head back home. No one really noticed because everyone wants to talk and not listen and also if you have always been a quiet person people sort of stop noticing you. Trying to find answers on the Internet just made me feel worse.

Now watching Amma and Appa; seeing Shakuntala Akka's tears; reading Surendran and Kapil's posts... I knew what I had done was a huge mistake. I was not invisible. I was just not reaching out and they did not know what was happening to me.

It's funny, a year ago I was running away from life and now I miss being alive. I want to play chess with Appa; bug Shakuntala Akka into making me pasta; sit with Kapil arguing about cricket; make Amma laugh; work on a quiz with Surendran; solve maths problems... there were so many good things in my life, I just forgot to count them.

Sitting there like a smoky cloud, I let my brain control the laptop and checked what Kapil was up to to find that he hadn't posted much, but then he never did like Facebook. Kapil would rather be out in the park kicking a football than taking selfies. As always Ashit's page was full of photos to prove how popular he was and what a hit he was at parties, often with Namita pouting next to him, looking like a brainless goldfish. It was as if there was nothing more to life than partying.

Why is it no one admits that parties get boring after a while? And that the music is kept so absurdly loud because few of the kids have anything to say. All conversation dies out soon enough and then you grin inanely and dance, trying desperately to prove you are having fun. Why is fun so important?

I remember a day I was with Kapil and Surendran preparing for a quiz, talking and arguing, flipping through big, fat books and when I looked at my watch it was evening. The hours had zipped by and I had been happy. There were so many happy times that I took for granted, and instead kept brooding over my few Facebook friends. All I thought about was the bad times, going over and over the things those bullies said. I am not stupid; at the back of my mind I knew I had to talk to someone and I know Appa would have listened and taken me seriously.

Time has a different pace now and I seem to come and go without being conscious of it. At times days pass without my knowing. One minute I was at my laptop and then it was the next morning and Appa was sitting with his coffee and newspaper in the veranda. So I decided to go to school by our bus. At the stop, I saw the girl and her father and now I could eavesdrop. They were arguing about some film that they had seen; she had liked it and he thought it was silly. It was very like the arguments we would have coming back in the car from the movie hall. Amma declaring that the Star Wars movies were made by adults who never grew up; Appa and me talking about fantasy and creativity; and her sarcastic laugh. At one point I used to talk to them all the time, why did I stop?

Riding in the school bus with no one looking at me was an interesting feeling. Here I was entering school and I wasn't anxiously looking around for Ashit and his gang. They were huddled by the basketball court and I floated up to listen to them. I know that bullies like Ashit and Namita never change; so who were they targeting now? My death would not have changed them because in their eyes it was somehow my fault. I was 'weak' and Ashit was 'toughening' me up. Once when Kapil had confronted them Ashit had drawled, 'What's the problem, bro? Are you so weak you can't take a little teasing?'

Teasing? He had dropped my books in a toilet and he had me by the neck, telling me to flush it when Kapil had come to the rescue.

As I listened to them, I froze. They were talking

about Kapil and Surendran. Ashit was furious at the way they had openly called him a bully and even used a hashtag.

'They can't get away with this,' he waved an angry hand. 'No one insults me and gets away. No one.'

Namita looked bored. 'What will you do? This is not Dhani, they will complain. Dhani never said a word but they will.' Then she laughed. 'HashtagAshitShetty thebully.'

He gave her a weird, sideways look, 'I have a plan but you'll have to help.'

'What?'

'Go and complain to Tripathi and make sure our principal believes you. You know, look very upset, cry a little, you can do that…'

Namita frowned, 'What are you talking about?'

'Tell him that Kapil and Surendran have been stalking you, making nasty comments, following you from school…' he shrugged. 'You know what I mean…'

Namita stared at him, suddenly going pale, and her eyes had widened as if Ashit's words had shocked her. 'And when he finds out that I'm lying? I'll be the one who will be thrown out of school, you idiot!' And she began to walk away looking furious.

'Aw c'mon!' Ashit called out after her.

To my surprise she did not turn back. 'No, I won't do it,' she said over her shoulder. 'No way! You forget

Dhani killed himself because of us.' She kept walking as Ashit shrugged, looking a bit shamefaced and then away.

Namita Panandikar standing up to Ashit and even remembering me! I should have been alive to see this day. As they walked away, I thought, I have to do something to stop Ashit from ruining more lives. I knew him too well. He was not going to stop. But what can a weird, floating ectoplasm like me do?

By then I was going past the staff room—the sanctum sanctorum where we kids were rarely allowed in—but now no one could stop me. I hovered by the table where two of my favourite teachers were sitting. There was Miss Menon, short hair, thick framed glasses and crisp words who taught maths, and Mr Bharve, thin and lanky, speaking with a lazy drawl who taught physics. They were fantastic teachers and they often called me in class. Miss Menon had a pile of notebooks on the table before her and was marking them, going tick… tick… slash… with a slight frown.

'Which class?' Bharve asked.

'Eleven B.'

'That was the class where Dhananjay… I heard about the scholarship.'

Menon nodded. 'All through class I was thinking of him. He had real talent in maths and he had a career there. His parents would have made sure he did well.'

'Why did he do it? Do you know?'

She gave a slow sad shake of her head, 'I wish I knew. I heard there was some problem with some boys bullying him.'

'Ashit Shetty?'

She nodded. 'I just wish he had made a formal complaint. Then I would have taken on Ashit and his father.'

'You would have been wasting your time. I have complained twice to Tripathi about Ashit but no action was taken, you know what he is like. If there are complaints Tripathi summons Ashit's father who comes in his latest luxury car, pulls out his cheque book and makes a big donation and everything is forgotten. That boy should be asked to leave; he is a danger to other students.'

'That won't happen and Ashit knows that.' Menon picked up her pen. 'Dhananjay was such a gentle kid.'

'Teenagers! I'll never understand them.'

Menon gave a small smile, 'You were a teenager once.'

Bharve laughed, 'The worst years of my life. I was convinced I'd be a failure at everything I tried to do.'

In the bus going back home I began to worry. I was always very good at that—anticipating problems that never happened. I looked out of the window as we sat in a traffic jam and brooded. Even Menon and Bharve can't control Ashit and his dad. There was always the danger that Namita could change her mind and complain against Kapil and Surendran. I have to find a way to stop Ashit. Permanently.

Then I thought, 'This is my fight and I can do anything I want. You can't suspend a ghost, can ya?' I felt amazingly free and calm.

Next morning, I was back in school after a night spent worrying about how to protect Kapil and Surendran from Ashit. What could I do? No one can see or hear me, so I can't warn them but I had a vague plan and it had to do with Facebook.

For the next two days I hovered around Ashit, listening to him talk. I discovered what a swollen head he had, showing off non-stop. He never stopped boasting about his father's fleet of luxury cars, their holidays abroad, his new iPhone or fancy ripped jeans or shoes, and his chamchas laughed obediently at his lame jokes. One thing made me hopeful. I noticed that Namita did not join them in the cafeteria even once, instead she sat with a bunch of girls looking glum.

That night I noticed that a funny thing was happening to my Facebook page. My profile photo was beginning to fade, turning into a grey smudge and even my name was turning hazy. When I posted a line as a test it still remained smudged so that you couldn't make out who had sent the post. An idea began to grow in my head because it looked like I was really turning into a social media spook.

So I posted my first comment, tagging all my friends in class and then I thought, this needs a name. Looking at my wavy, hazy, swirling face, I signed off 'Ectoplasm'. Surendran would get the joke.

Post 1: Do the students of Class XI B know that our super rich Ashit Shetty steals cash from his Dad's wallet? Signed Ectoplasm

I followed that up with more posts in the next couple of days.

Post 2: Ashit Shetty got 9 out of 50 in the last maths test and he has two tutors. What a genius! Signed Ectoplasm

Then I followed him home a couple of times, listening to people talk and learning more. Now the posts came every day about Ashit being thrown out of two schools, his lying to teachers and so on; as the class whispered and giggled Ashit began to look more and more haunted, constantly checking his phone and lurking in the shadows.

Post 7: Ashit Shetty got drunk and crashed his father's new Porsche that cost 2 crores. Signed Ectoplasm

Then I moved in for the kill.

Post 8: Ashit Shetty wanted Namita Panandikar to make a false complaint of harassment against two boys in their class because they called him a bully.

Way to go, Ashit! Let the girls fight your battles. Signed Ectoplasm

Next morning, Ashit's father drove into school in his chauffeur-driven BMW and marched into Tripathi's room and I followed. He crashed the door shut as I slid in behind him and immediately began yelling, leaning across the table as our brave principal cowered in his chair. It was all about the lakhs of rupees that he had donated to the school. How Ashit was a gentle, well-behaved boy... at which even Tripathi bravely shook his head in disagreement.

Mr Shetty loomed over Tripathi, nose to nose, yelling, 'You took five lakhs in cash for yourself to give him admission! Want me to tell the school board about it?'

'No... no Mr Shetty...' Tripathi mumbled.

'Then fix this!'

As Shetty strode out, I caught a glimpse of Ashit standing in the corridor and he had a nasty smirk on his face.

A grim Tripathi emerged from his office. Now he had his Boss face on. He marched into the staff room and as I was right behind him the door swung right through me, an ectoplasmic collision that I did not feel at all.

Tripathi announced to a row of curious faces, 'This bullying on social media of Ashit Shetty has to stop immediately. His father was here just now complaining how it was making the poor boy depressed…'

The teachers stared at him in silence.

Tripathi's voice got louder, 'We have to find out who is responsible. I cannot allow any bullying in school.'

The silence was broken by a laugh, I turned to see that Miss Menon was laughing. 'Ashit Shetty? Poor boy?'

Then Mr Bharve spoke up, followed by Mrs Kumar, Mr Roy and Miss Pandit.

'He is the bully, Mr Tripathi. Most of the junior kids are scared of him.'

'I have complained so many times but no action has been taken.'

'He disrupts my class, never submits his assignments, is rude…'

The other teachers were nodding in agreement. Bharve walked up to Tripathi. 'Where were you when Dhananjay killed himself? I had mentioned the episode in the cafeteria and Kapil Sinha told you about the scene in the toilet…'

My heart soared. They had noticed and spoken up. Kapil had not let me down.

'No one listened to the boy who was truly bullied,' Menon had joined Bharve. 'Was it because his father did not donate lakhs to the school?'

'Dhananjay never complained to me,' Tripathi protested in a small voice.

'But we did!'

Post 9: Ashit Shetty's father donates money to the school so his son can stay. Bully father has a stupid son. Signed Ectoplasm

I watched Tripathi call Ashit's father and tell him that he could not help anymore. All the teachers had complained to the school board and many had threatened to resign. The anonymous Facebook posts could not be cyber bullying as what the posts said were all true. Then Tripathi told Shetty about me and I got a feeling Ashit's father had not known about that, because he did not call again.

Ashit stopped coming to school. Lurking in the classroom, I heard that he was being sent to some fancy residential school in the hills. My job was done. Kapil and Surendran were safe. Now this ectoplasm was going to vanish from Facebook.

BASHEER'S GHOSTLY PULAO

Dinner was over at the haveli of Nawab Karimullah Khan and it was time for the paan and the hookah to be served.

Nawab Jahandar Khan took a slow puff at his hookah and said, 'Ah, my friend Karim! Next time I visit Delhi I'll surely take you with me.'

His best friend Karimullah popped a paan into his mouth and frowned. 'Why is that? I have been to Delhi many times and I prefer my city of Lucknow.'

'Of course! Lucknow is far superior as a city but there is one thing,' Jahandar raised his forefinger, 'one thing, that Delhi does better.'

Everyone in the baithak, the haveli's sitting room, leaned forward eagerly to discover what could be this mysterious Delhi thing. Asad and Basheer were standing at the door and the khansama Baqar Ali was stationed behind the two nawabs, who sat leaning against bolsters on the carpet. What could be so good in Delhi?

Karimullah stopped chewing. 'Better than Lucknow?'

'Ah yes!' Jahandar gave a dreamy smile. 'It's the way the bawarchis of Delhi cook rice. Such amazing recipes!'

'Rice?' Karimullah looked puzzled, 'just *rice*?'

'I'm talking of the biryani of Delhi,' Jahandar waved a hand in the air. 'Aha aha… what taste! What aroma! The meat is cooked to become soft as velvet. Our Lucknow pulaos don't even come close to their biryanis.'

There was a deathly silence in the room as everyone stared at Jahandar in shock. How could he say such a thing? He had just eaten a grand Lucknowi meal where Asad the chef had served his delicious lamb pulao with cinnamon, and here he was praising a biryani! Basheer took a quick look at his brother's face but Asad just looked calm and politely interested. However, Karimullah was not going to take it quietly if anyone criticized the food he offered to his guests.

He stared grimly at his friend and asked carefully, 'Are you saying, Jahandar, that you prefer a Delhi biryani to our pulao?'

'Yes I do! My friends took me to the food shop of Majid Mian in the shadows of the Jama Masjid and there I tasted outstanding biryanis made with mutton, chicken and even vegetables. A variety I have never had before.'

Karimullah leaned forward. 'I'm sure the biryanis were good but how can they be better than our Moti Pulao, Chameli Pulao, Zafrani Pulao…'

Jahandar waved a disdainful hand in the air. 'Compared to biryanis, our pulaos taste quite bland.'

'Our pulaos are subtle!' Karimullah gave his friend a fierce slit-eyed look. It was the look that made Basheer shake in his shoes because it meant that Nawabsaab was about to lose his temper. 'I DO NOT AGREE!' and his voice began to rise. 'Nothing can match the delectable taste of our pulaos! They are the finest creations of the chefs of Awadh.'

Jahandar enjoyed teasing his quick-tempered friend and so with a crooked smile he said, 'Even our King Wajid Ali Shah would agree with me if he ate at Majid Mian's food shop.' Then he needled on, 'I have got a new chef, Maqsood Ali, straight from the galis of Chandni Chowk, who is now serving up a variety of Delhi dishes at my dastarkhwan. As a matter of fact, why don't you come and taste them? I'm inviting you and Begum Sahiba to dinner this Sunday and you'll know what I'm talking about.'

Karimullah was still looking angry. 'Then why don't we have both a biryani and a pulao on the menu? My bawarchi Asad Mian will make a special pulao and we'll taste both. Our guests will then decide which is better.'

'Ah! A contest! What a wonderful idea!'

'Be prepared to lose, Jahandar! No one can compete with my ala bawarchi Asad Mian. He has been trained by my former chef, the legendary Ustad Kallu!' He waved towards Asad standing at the door, who bowed with a small smile, and Basheer in a fit of nervousness, bowed too.

So that's how it started, the great Pulao-Biryani Battle that became the talk of the town in Lucknow.

෴

All this was happening in the nineteenth century in the city of Lucknow, the capital of the kingdom of Awadh. The ruler was Nawab Wajid Ali Shah who enjoyed all the good things in life—poetry, music, dance and of course good food. And following his lead so did the noblemen. They were all very proud of their kitchens headed by famous chefs called bawarchis who prepared all kinds of delectable dishes. Every nawab was convinced his bawarchi was the best.

Karimullah Khan's kitchen was once run by the famous chef Ustad Kallu, and his pulaos, kalias, kormas and many types of kababs were famous across the city. They said that his gilouti kabab could make people feel they had tasted a slice of the food of jannat, or heaven. Then the young and talented Asad Mian had to take over in a hurry one morning when, while stirring a handi of dal, Ustad Kallu fainted and then died. His assistant Asad, though very young, had to take over immediately and he had continued with Ustad's style of cooking. Soon guests were talking of his delicious mutton pasanda—a roasted leg of lamb; his sweet zarda rice and creamy phirni with almonds and of course his pulaos and kababs.

Basheer was Asad's younger brother. The brothers had started to work very young when their father died. Basheer was just eleven when he began as a degshor, or the boy who cleaned all the pots and pans. Now at fifteen he had been promoted to the job of the masalchi, grinding and mixing the masalas for each dish. It was a very important job. If the correct spices were not chosen in the right measurement and then ground properly, then a dish could be ruined. Basheer had to learn all about spices—when to use the green or the brown cardamom; the red or green chillies; which dish required coriander or cumin; fenugreek or asafoetida. He loved the subtle aroma of cinnamon, cloves, nutmeg and mace that went into the garam masala. Asad had promised that soon he would start teaching him to cook.

⚜

The morning after the Biryani-Pulao contest was declared, Asad was summoned by Nawabsaab for what Basheer thought of as a war council. The battle between

Lucknow's pulao and Delhi's biryani had to be won by the pulao, whatever the cost.

As Asad walked to the baithak the kitchen staff followed behind him. There was Bilal, the junior bawarchi, the post Asad had held under Ustad Kallu. He made the simpler dishes like dals, vegetables and various kinds of breads. Next walked Basheer the masalchi, followed by Chhuttan who did all the vegetable chopping and peeling, and right behind strolled Shabbo who had taken over from Basheer as the degshor and spent his day scrubbing a mountain of pots and pans.

They all stopped at the door as Asad went in and bowed before Karimullah who was smoking a hookah and reading some papers.

'Huzoor.'

'Ah, Asad! You know what happened last night, don't you?'

'I do, huzoor.' Then Asad took out a small chit of paper from his kurta pocket. 'I have made a list of all the pulaos that I learnt from Ustad Kallu and you can choose which one I should prepare for Sunday's dinner.' Nawabsaab waved a gracious hand, so Asad continued, 'There is the Gulzar pulao, Nur, Koku, Moti, Chameli, Mutanjan, Anardana, Nauratan... each cooked in a different blend of ingredients.'

'Wait!' Karimullah who had been listening rather sleepily suddenly sat up. 'I have thought of something!

Remember that pulao... what was it called? Ustad made it just once... Oh yes! Pulao Lajawab. My guests loved it. Make that.'

'Pulao Lajawab?' Asad looked a little anxious. 'Huzoor, I saw him make that only once. You know he died suddenly. I'm not very sure of the recipe... as a matter of fact I never even tasted it.'

'I'm sure if you tried you can remember it.' Karimullah laughed. 'I want you to make the Pulao Lajawab. You'll get it right, I know.'

They all trooped back to the kitchen in silence. Pulao Lajawab? Bilal and Basheer had never heard of it. Reaching the kitchen, Asad collapsed on a bench and brooded, then he pulled out his scrap of paper and a pencil and began to scribble, occasionally shaking his head and scratching out something as he tried to list the ingredients—basmati rice, mutton pieces, saffron, cardamom, cinnamon...

'I have a vague memory of Ustad saying that this pulao was different because it used some expensive ingredients. He went off to the bazaar to order them. Oh what were they?'

Just then Gulabo, Begum Sahiba's maid, came into the kitchen to collect the breakfast for her mistress and seeing their glum faces asked, 'Now what's the matter?'

'You know,' Basheer explained, 'about the Pulao-Biryani battle, don't you?'

'Of course! Begum Sahiba's already planning what she will wear on Sunday.' She gave a small satisfied smile. 'I'm going with her of course.' Then she turned to Asad, 'So why are you looking so worried?'

'Nawabsaab wants the Pulao Lajawab,' Asad explained. 'And I have never cooked it. You know what Ustad Kallu was like. He hated sharing recipes and I usually learned the recipes by watching him cook. If I asked any questions he would just shout at me.'

'It must have been really hard for you,' Bilal said. 'I am so happy you teach me, Asad Ustad.'

'You never saw him cook this pulao?' Chhuttan asked.

'He cooked it only once and that morning I was busy cooking other dishes. I thought I'd learn the next time…'

'And then he fell into the pot of dal and died,' little Shabbo said with gloomy satisfaction.

'Well not exactly *fell into* the pot…' Asad corrected him. 'He sort of sprawled over it and we all ran and pulled him away.'

There was a moment's silence as they all remembered Ustad Kallu. He was a short, stocky, bad-tempered man who snapped at everyone. He sweated a lot while cooking and had a large towel slung over his shoulder to wipe his face. After his work was done he would sit under a tree outside the kitchen door chewing paan and spitting paan juice as he lectured everyone. Asad had to be very patient and polite to become his trusted assistant.

Basheer followed Gulabo with a tray of food into the haveli. It had rooms built around two open courtyards with a veranda running in front. The first courtyard was the mardana where all the men stayed—Nawabsaab, his sons, brothers and nephews. The second courtyard was the zenana where all the women lived. Here the women stepped behind a curtain whenever men who were not family members entered, because of the rules of the purdah. Begum Sahiba often checked about the kitchen when he came to deliver the food and so Basheer was familiar with Begum Sahiba's voice behind a chik curtain but he had never seen her face. He heard she was beautiful and he knew she was very kind.

Gulabo carried the trays inside and said, 'Wait a moment, Basheer. Begum Sahiba wants to talk to you.' Basheer knew what she wanted to ask.

The chik curtain over the door was lowered and he heard the clink of bangles as Begum Sahiba came to stand on the other side. Basheer bowed with an adaab as he got a whiff of the attar perfume she was wearing. It was jasmine today.

'Asad must be busy cooking lunch so I thought I'd ask you.'

'Ji Begum Sahiba.'

'I heard about Sunday's dinner. Has Asad decided which pulao he will cook?'

'Huzoor, Bhaiya wanted to make the Mutanjan Pulao but Nawabsaab wants the Pulao Lajawab.'

'Pulao Lajawab?' her voice was puzzled.

'It seems Ustad Kallu only made it once. He had learnt the recipe recently and then umm…'

'He died.' There was a small silence and then she said, 'Oh I remember now! It was really delicious and quite unusual. It was a recipe from Kashmir.'

'Huzoor…' Basheer began a little nervously. 'May I ask you something?'

'Of course!'

'You see, Ustad Kallu never taught Bhaiya any recipe. Bhaiya had to learn by watching him cook and he saw Ustad cook this pulao just once.'

There was a puzzled silence across the curtain. Then, 'So what's the problem?'

'He can't remember all the ingredients. He says there were some special ones that were very expensive and had to be ordered at the bazaar. Huzoor, would you remember what they were?'

Behind the curtain he heard her ask Gulabo to get her a stool to sit on. 'Get me a mura, Gulabo. This is going to take some time.' Then, always kind and thoughtful, she said to Basheer, 'You sit down too, beta.' So Basheer sat cross-legged on the floor before a curtain, talking to a woman he had never seen. 'It was a very special occasion,' she said with a nostalgic sigh. 'Our eldest son's marriage was being fixed and the Nawab of Rampur was coming to dinner.'

'Rampur! They have a famous royal kitchen!'

'Exactly! So we had to serve a really good meal. Nawabsaab and I discussed the menu with Ustad Kallu. When we came to the pulao he suggested this new pulao recipe that he had found.'

'It was good?'

'Oh it was sublime… such a subtle mix of flavours and with a hint of sweetness to balance the rich spices…'

'And the ingredients, huzoor?' he reminded her gently.

'Oh I wish I could remember! Ustad went to the bazaar and ordered them at Dinanath's grocery shop in Aminabad. Something… oh, what were they? Gulqand… no no… you don't use rose jam in pulao. Was it raisins from Kabul? Saffron from Kashmir?' she sighed. 'I'm sorry beta, but I can't remember. I know it was expensive because Nawabsaab protested a bit but Ustad Kallu insisted.'

A disappointed Basheer went back to the kitchen and told Asad, 'Begum Sahiba only remembers the recipe was from Kashmir and it was delicious, nothing else.'

Just then Baqar Ali, Nawabsaab's khansama came busily in to collect his master's breakfast. Asad and

Baqar Ali did not get along because when Ustad Kallu died, the khansama wanted his nephew to head the kitchen. That way uncle and nephew could run the haveli, but Nawabsaab had chosen Asad. Baqar Ali had never forgiven Asad for that. Now he collected the tray of food and Basheer followed carrying a plate of sliced fruits and a jug of water. Usually this was a silent trip as the khansama was too snooty to talk to a mere masalchi, but today Baqar Ali was in a mood to chat.

'So how is the plan for Sunday's pulao going, Basheer?' Baqar Ali was suddenly being very friendly, 'The Pulao Lajawab?'

'Very well,' said Basheer shortly, knowing full well that nothing would make the khansama happier than if Asad's pulao lost to a mere biryani.

'I hope so! You know that Nawabsaab does not like losing a bet.'

'I do.'

'Haveli ki izzat ka sawaal hai,' Baqar Ali said solemnly, 'it is a matter of the honour of this haveli.'

'I know.' Basheer was not keen to talk but Baqar Ali was not done yet.

'Today is Thursday, when will you shop for the spices?'

'Soon.'

'Oh, doesn't Asad Mian know what he has to buy?'

'He does. We'll shop in time.'

'Good! I am very pleased,' said Baqar Ali, sounding very superior.

Who cares? Basheer thought rebelliously.

Back in the kitchen, Basheer got his breakfast—a bowl of steaming nihari soup and a sheermal bread left over from last night's dinner—and sat in a patch of watery sun outside the kitchen. Dipping a piece of sheermal into the nihari, he munched and thought about what Baqar Ali had said. Suddenly he froze.

In all the excitement he had forgotten something! Thinking of Baqar Ali made him remember.

Ustad Kallu's ghost!

Just because he had died did not mean that Ustad Kallu was going to give up being a chef. Right after his death he had begun to haunt his kitchen and for some strange reason he had only chosen to speak to Basheer.

For days Basheer had Ustad Kallu yelling into his ears about masala and grinding and how Basheer was a terrible masalchi. He wondered why Kallu was hanging around the kitchen only to bug him and not the others. Then one day Kallu told him of his problem. Nawabsaab was keen to help Kallu's widow and had given a bag full of coins to Baqar Ali to give to her, but instead the greedy khansama had kept the money. Hearing this, Basheer had told Asad, managing to hide the fact that he had heard it from a ghost. Asad had found a clever way to let Nawabsaab know that Kallu's widow needed help and had not received any money.

What followed made the whole kitchen celebrate. A furious Nawabsaab had summoned Baqar Ali and given him such a yelling the walls of the baithak shook. The khansama was forced to give the bag of coins to Asad and they had given it to the widow. This was another reason why Baqar Ali's nephew did not get the chef's job.

The problem was that since then, the ghost had never spoken to Basheer again.

'I have to get the ghost back,' Basheer thought, 'only Ustad can give us the correct recipe and how to cook it.'

Chewing away, he planned on a way to call back the ghost. Now what was he doing when Ustad Kallu first spoke angrily into his ear?

'I was peeling garlic for a korma,' he remembered, 'and Ustad thought I was taking too many of them.' He remembered how the extra garlic pods began to float in the air and scared him to death. Basheer grinned at the memory. 'Nothing got Ustad so angry as a wrong masala mix and lazy cooking.'

Basheer knew what he had to do. He had to mess up a masala, and if the ghost was still around then he was sure Ustad would lose his temper and yell into Basheer's ear. So far he had been the perfect masalchi but today he was going to do everything wrong. He would go on messing up till Ustad was forced to reveal his recipe of Pulao Lajawab.

It was time to fix the menu of the day and Bilal, Chhuttan and Basheer went to Asad for instructions. It was always Asad who decided what would be cooked for lunch or dinner, unless any family member sent in a request. Most mornings Asad snapped out the instructions but this morning he looked worried and absent-minded.

He scratched his chin. 'Umm… Bilal for lunch you make a masoor dal…'

'We had masoor dal yesterday,' Bilal said.

'Oh right! Then make arhar dal with a tadka of spices in ghee; a raita with onions, some plain rotis. I'll make a cabbage and potato sabji, and as last night's meal was very rich, just a simple keema curry with peas—and fry a few boti kababs.'

'I'll start the dal,' Bilal hurried away.

'I'll start chopping the onions and cabbage,' Chhuttan went off to his chopping board.

'Basheer…' Asad looked absently at him.

'Ground ginger and garam masala for the cabbage,' Basheer began as Asad nodded. 'Ground onions, ginger and garlic, whole garam masala, chopped coriander leaves and sliced chillies for the keema curry…'

'And for the kababs?'

'Yoghurt beaten smooth, then spiced with cinnamon powder, pepper and salt to marinate the kababs.'

'Right!' Asad waved him away.

Basheer headed for his corner of the kitchen where his grinding stone and iron mortar and pestle sat on a shelf next to a marble chopping board with his knives. In front of the board were baskets of onions, ginger, coriander leaves, chillies and garlic. He took a plate and headed for the store room to collect all the ingredients for the garam masala. When he came back there were cloves, cardamom, cinnamon and pepper on the plate, but ignoring what Ustad Kallu had taught him, there was no nutmeg or mace. As he had planned, for the first time Basheer was about to ruin his garam masala.

With a thudding heart Basheer solemnly put the spices in the pestle and then he felt a small disapproving breeze begin to swirl around his head as his ears began to feel oddly cold.

'Ustad?' he whispered hopefully, 'You there?'

He waited a while but the ghost remained stubbornly silent. So with a disappointed sigh Basheer went back to the store room and got the missing spices, and after adding the mace and nutmeg he began to pound away. Then he ground the ginger on the grinding stone and put the powdered masala and ginger on a plate which he left beside Asad where he was already frying chopped onions.

As he went past him, Chhuttan, who was slicing cabbages at high speed, muttered, 'He's really worried.'

'Very. If he doesn't get it right you know what Baqar Ali will do. Once again he'll start whispering to Nawabsaab about his wonderful nephew.'

'I wish there was a way to talk to Ustad Kallu!'

'I wish,' Basheer said grimly.

As he began peeling and chopping onions for the keema curry, Basheer thought, 'The first time Ustad Kallu's ghost spoke to me it was because of the garlic. He thought I had taken too many.' So next to the earthy brown ginger and the pink onions he laid out a huge pile of creamy garlic pods. 'Let's see if this makes that mad cook yell at me. So much garlic is sure to ruin a curry.' Then trying to look casual, humming under his breath, he went on chopping the onions.

Right before his eyes half the garlic pods floated up in the air and went back to the basket. Basheer promptly put them back on the chopping board again. Now it felt like there was a small storm blowing in his corner of the kitchen. The whooshing sound kept getting louder and louder and his hair was beginning to stand on end.

'Say something, Ustad,' he pleaded in a low voice. 'Please talk to me. I really need your help.' His nose was icy cold but sadly there was no one speaking into his ears.

'Oye idiot!' Asad yelled from across the kitchen, making Basheer jump. 'What are you doing? Why have you taken so much garlic? This is a keema curry, not a korma.' Basheer looked up feeling a bit confused as the air quietened again and the ghost seemed to vanish. 'Less garlic! Are you listening to me?'

'Ji Bhaiya,' Basheer said apologetically, 'sorry for the mistake.' And he put away the extra garlic pods. 'He is definitely here,' Basheer thought. 'But he's not interested in talking to me. I have to do something that will make him so angry that he wouldn't be able to resist shouting at me.' He brooded away, 'The garlic trick won't do. What can I do to make Ustad Kallu truly and absolutely hopping mad?'

An hour later Basheer was heading for the store room again to get some green chillies and turmeric when he glanced out of the kitchen door and saw Chhuttan taking a break, standing in the sun smoking a biri. In a blinding flash he knew what he had to try next.

For Ustad Kallu there were two sacred spaces in his life—the kitchen and the store room. You had to take a bath before you could enter the kitchen and you had to keep all the pots and pans, the ladles and spatulas sparkling clean. Similarly, you took off your shoes before entering the store room. Inside, every item had to be kept in the right place. On the floor were jute sacks with the rice and wheat. On the shelves were the glass jars, big and small, holding various kinds of dals and spices. The onions, ginger, garlic and fresh vegetables sat in open baskets and the pickles were kept in a row of white and brown martbaan ceramic jars.

Basheer pushed back the store room door with a bang, hoping to catch Ustad's attention, and then stamped in wearing his dusty leather chappals. Immediately an angry breeze whooshed in after him. Standing in the middle of the store room Basheer reached into his kurta pocket and pulled out a biri and a box of matches that he had borrowed from Chhuttan.

Then defiantly he said into the whirling air around him, 'Want a biri, Ustad?'

Now there was a chattering noise in his ears like a bunch of crows arguing but he heard no words.

Basheer held up the matches. 'Either you talk or I smoke a stinking biri in the store room. Right next to the masalas. Your choice, Ustad.'

Silence.

'What's the problem, Ustad? You forgot how to talk? Never had that problem before.' Basheer was really having fun being rude.

Basheer's head was now in the middle of a tornado of noise and whirling air and he began to feel even colder. He pulled out a match stick, stuck a biri between his lips and was about to light it when...

'Theek hai... theek hai... no more drama. Talk!'

'Oh Allah is great!' Basheer breathed in relief. 'Ustad, Bhaiya needs the recipe of the Pulao Lajawab. You see what happened when Nawab Jahandar Khan came to dinner yesterday…' in his excitement Basheer was starting to sound very confused.

'I heard.'

'Bhaiya can't remember the recipe.'

'I heard him. He remembers the recipe just fine. Nothing wrong with it.'

'Are you sure? Begum Sahiba says that you said it was a Kashmiri recipe and there were some unusual ingredients that you had to order at Dinanath's grocery store and…' he stopped for breath, 'they were very expensive and Begum Sahiba said that Nawabsaab…'

There was a small silence as if Ustad Kallu was not too keen to reveal his culinary secrets. Then he said reluctantly, 'It was a long time ago. I don't remember everything; there were dried plums and apricots, raisins from Kabul, saffron from Kashmir…' and Basheer could hear him chewing.

'Are you chewing paan, Ustad?' he asked in surprise.

'Yes I am. What's wrong with that? I'm not smoking a biri near the masalas like you. You are the stupidest masalchi I have ever seen. No masalchi ever…'

'I know, I know,' Basheer tried to soothe him. 'I was just trying to make you talk. You know I would never fill the store room with tobacco smoke.'

In reply he heard Ustad Kallu spit out the paan juice, and to Basheer's amazement tiny spots of red appeared on the front of his white kurta.

'You are spitting on me, Ustad?' he asked, feeling very hurt. 'How can you? I am your student, you taught me…'

'Because you are…' and off went Ustad Kallu using the choicest abuses, 'Bewaqoof! Badmaash! Badtameez!!'

'Yes… yes…' Basheer tried to calm him down, 'have another paan. One more question. Begum Sahiba said it is a Kashmiri recipe. Did you get the recipe from a Kashmiri cook here in Lucknow?'

'Of course! My wife! Who else? She is from Kashmir and her father was a famous cook and this is her family recipe. Don't you know anything?'

'So if we ask her she'll teach Bhaiya?'

'Of course she will. She loves Asad because he gave her the money and even now he visits her and takes care of her. Unlike you! You ungrateful wretch!'

'Oh good!' Basheer grinned into the space around him as the buzzing in his ears became softer. 'Thank you so much, Ustad, I really apologize for bothering you but Bhaiya's job is at stake. If he loses this contest then Baqar Ali will again try to get Nawabsaab to sack him.'

'Curse that stupid khansama!'

'One final question, Ustad…'

'What now?'

'They have paan in jannat? I thought heaven only had pulaos and kheer.'

The air around his head seemed to stiffen and then Basheer felt as if someone had hit him hard across the back of his head.

'OOF!' He decided he wouldn't ask if the djinns smoked biris.

'Go and help Asad,' Ustad Kallu's voice was beginning to fade away as Basheer came out of the store room. 'And Basheer, if I ever see a biri in your hand I'll come back and spit on your face!'

'Never, Ustad! I swear! No biris ever!' Basheer promised, hurrying to the kitchen. He absently looked down at the front of his kurta and discovered that the red spots had vanished.

For the rest of the day Basheer brooded over how to tell Asad what Ustad Kallu had told him without revealing that he was talking to a ghost. His brother was a practical man who said ghosts and djinns were nonsense. He would not believe that the ghost of a dead chef had spoken into Basheer's ear. He could also hit Basheer for making up a story, and one hard slap on the head was enough for one day. Ustad Kallu had hit him so hard Basheer had really seen stars at day time.

That night as they headed home, Basheer looked up at Asad. 'Bhaiya, I have been thinking…' he began carefully.

'Since when can you think?' Asad asked, amused. 'You just know how to mix masala.'

'Oof! Listen na... I was thinking of what Begum Sahiba said to me today about the Pulao Lajawab.'

'What?' Asad's steps slowed.

'She said it was a Kashmiri dish and you told me once that Ustad Kallu got many recipes from his wife because she came from a family of Kashmiri cooks.'

'Yes I know. They are called wazas and they cook an amazing meal of over thirty dishes called a wazwan. There is the rista, the tabak maaz, the gushtaba...' Asad went on dreamily.

Basheer interrupted him, '... and if she taught Ustad then she would know the recipe of the pulao?'

For the first time that day Asad began to smile. 'That is a very clever idea Basheer! We'll go and visit her early tomorrow morning on the way to work.'

The sun was still hidden behind the floating mist when the brothers wrapped in shawls headed for the home of Gauhar Bi, the widow of Ustad Kallu. Usually Basheer hated getting up early in winter and having to crawl out from under the quilt, but today he was so excited he nearly forgot to comb his hair.

Opening the door Gauhar Bi's eyes widened and she smiled in delight. 'Asad! Basheer! How lovely to see you.'

Asad followed her into the kitchen where she was

heating milk on the angeethi. She poured the milk into three glasses and stirred in the sugar and ground almonds. Then they all sat around the glowing kitchen fire sipping the drink as Asad told her about the Pulao-Biryani contest.

Gauhar Bi laughed, the wrinkles around her large eyes deepening in amusement, 'A biryani better than our pulao? Impossible!'

Asad recited the list of ingredients for the pulao and asked, 'Have I forgotten anything?'

'For the pulao you have everything but you need something to decorate it and that makes it so different.' Basheer and Asad leaned forward eagerly. 'You need the dry fruits of Kashmir and Kabul—plums, apricots, raisins, figs and fresh pomegranates. You fry the raisins, dried plums and apricots in ghee. You lay out the pulao on a silver salver and before serving you sprinkle the dry fruits and pomegranate seeds on top and then add a splash of rose water.'

'Ah! Fry the dried fruits in ghee! That was what I forgot!' Asad smiled in relief.

'And there is a trick with the masala,' Gauhar Bi continued. 'Put whole garam masala, some slices of onions and ginger into a cloth bag and put it into the water in which you are boiling the rice.'

'Of course! The Kashmiri yakhni. It makes the rice so fragrant.'

'Oh one more thing!' Gauhar Bi sat up. 'You do remember about the milk and oranges, don't you?'

Basheer raised his head, 'Milk?'

Asad's eyes were wide with surprise, 'Oranges in pulao?'

'Oh, it's a little trick my father had. When you are putting the pulao to steam in a dum you add half a cup of cold milk mixed with the juice of one orange. The flavour blends beautifully with the saffron.'

As they were leaving, the gentle old lady stood at the door, 'Come back and tell me how you won because I am absolutely sure you will. My husband loved you two like his own sons.'

'Oranges? Milk? In pulao!' Asad mumbled. 'Who would have thought of that!'

Walking away, Basheer remembered the slap on his head and grinned, 'Ustad *loved* us like his sons? Really?'

Asad laughed. 'He had no sons. Do you think he would have taught me anything if he had a son? Only his son would have been taught the recipes and he would have taken over as the bawarchi at the haveli. I want to change that and that is why I am teaching Bilal.'

'Thank god for daughters!'

Feeling happy and carefree again the brothers walked to work.

လ⬥ၐ

It was Sunday evening and the Pulao Lajawab was ready. While it was cooking, the kitchen had filled with the delicious smells of spices, boiling rice and frying meat. The pulao had been cooked in two giant handis, and the kitchen staff had loaded them onto a horse cart. The pulao arrived at the haveli of Jahandar Khan an hour before dinner was to be served. The nawab's new chef Maqsood Ali was waiting at the kitchen door to welcome them.

Maqsood had prepared quite a spread. There was of course the biryani and with it a light mutton korma to be eaten with naan; shami kababs, a raita, salad and a phirni for dessert. Often at the feasts at the homes of nawabs over a dozen dishes would be served, but today the menu had been kept simple because all the guests had come to taste the pulao and biryani. Maqsood was a friendly man and soon he and Asad were discussing recipes and sharing cooking tips. Strangely, Basheer was not feeling anxious at all. His Bhaiya had done his best and now it was in the hands of Allah.

There were over twenty guests at the table, ten men in the mardana, their wives in the zenana and a few children. In the baithak the carpet had been covered by the bright dastarkhwan cloth and the men sat down to a grand meal. Two big silver platters piled high with pulao and biryani sat in the middle. The pulao's top glistened with the dried fruit and it was fragrant with rose water. The biryani smelled strongly of meat and spices with layers of rice in white and saffron. The guests began to eat and soon there were 'Wah! Wah!' for both the dishes and the platters emptied fast.

Once the meal was over and the dishes had been cleared away, the khansama and his assistants arrived with jars of water and towels for everyone to wash their hands and the dastarkhwan cloth was taken away. As the guests sat leaning against bolsters, the hookahs and silver platters of paan were brought in. The two chefs and their staff were all hovering at the door to hear the final verdict.

'Ah Karim, my friend!' Jahandar turned to Karimullah Khan. 'So what did you think of the Gosht ki Biryani?'

'It was delicious...' began Karimullah, making Basheer's heart sink. 'But Jahandar, will you honestly say that the pulao was any less delectable?'

Jahandar smiled back at his friend, 'I agree with you. Both were equally good. I was teasing you that night when I said that pulaos are bland. Pulaos and biryanis when cooked by our two talented chefs are the finest in Awadh.'

Asad and Maqsood exchanged a smiling glance. It was always like this in Delhi and Lucknow—no one said rude or critical words; they preferred to praise and encourage people. It was the Tehzeeb—the culture of the two great cities.

One guest laughed, 'Well, it did mean we all got an unforgettable meal.'

'Also,' Karimullah said gently, 'I have to confess that the pulao you ate was actually from Kashmir.'

'And,' Jahandar laughed, 'the biryani you so enjoyed was first created in Rampur. All our dishes are Hindustani.'

Then Asad and Maqsood were invited to meet the guests who praised their cooking, and each got a bag of clinking coins for them and their staff. A happy troupe of cooks and staff drifted back to the kitchen.

'Oof I'm so hungry!' Basheer exclaimed. 'Is there any pulao or biryani left? They all ate so much and the platters came back empty.'

Maqsood laughed, 'Don't you worry. I had kept aside everything for us. You are all invited to my kitchen for dinner.'

They all settled on the floor of the kitchen before the bowls and platters of food, and as Basheer bit into a shami kabab he thought he felt a soft hand touch his head in blessing. It felt like Ustad Kallu was saying a gentle goodbye.

'Who knows?' Basheer thought with a happy sigh, 'maybe Ustad did love us after all!'